AN *IN PLAIN SIGHT* PREQUEL NOVELLA

PROMISE ME Forever

ELICE NANGE

COPYRIGHT

DEDICATION

No matter how dark the night is, I will always come for you.
~ Dahlia Brewer

EXTRAS

Here ~ Alessia Cara
You Broke Me First ~ Tate McRae
Brokenhearted ~ Carly Rose
Kiss from a Rose ~ Seal
Knocking On My Heart ~ Frawley
I Was Made For Loving You ~ Tori Kelly & Ed Sheeran
Flashlight ~ Jessie J
I Didn't Know My Own Strength ~ Whitney Houston
Endless Love ~ Lionel Richie & Diana Ross
Always Remember Us This Way ~ Lady Gaga
Perfect ~ Ed Sheeran
Yours ~ Ella Henderson
IDGAF ~ Dua Lipa
People ~ Libianca
Everytime We Touch ~ Cascada

FOREWORD

Promise Me Forever is a dark contemporary romance novella with dark themes. It is a second chance, interracial, forbidden love, MMF, ménage/why choose, romantic suspense, dark mafia billionaire romance.

It contains no cheating and features a transgender side character. This story is darker than the previous three books in this series, contains harsh and insensitive language, and some aspects of it will make you uncomfortable. It also touches on several sensitive topics, including dysfunctional family dynamics, abusive parents, grief, loss, explicit sex, childhood neglect, murder (alluded to, non-graphic), violence, etc.

It depicts a breeding kink and a lactation kink.

Reader discretion is advised.

If dark and unconventional content triggers you, this isn't the book for you.

For a comprehensive list of content warnings, visit:
https://elicenange.com/promisemeforever/

BLURB

Absence doesn't make the heart grow fonder.
It only fills it with resentment and regret.

Nineteen years ago, I lost the love of my life for four dangerous reasons.
Power. Control. Money. Love.
These forces don't just break hearts; they shatter lives, and mine was no exception.
Left irreparably scarred, I vowed never to be vulnerable again.
I fortified my defective heart against heartbreak while channeling my energy into amassing an abundance of power, mastering control, and accumulating wealth.
Love?
It's a treacherous illusion, a game for fools; something I've become far too cynical to truly let it in.
That, and time doesn't heal all wounds. Far from it.
What I am is defective and proud. Having embraced my flaws, I wear my scars and cynicism defiantly, determined to live my life on my own terms — the best revenge to strive for.
Until an unconventional proposition slithers into my world, a dangerous and ill-timed offer in a treacherous game, but one impossible to ignore.
Turning it down was the most gut-wrenching decision I ever had to make, but I did so anyway — for her.
For the woman my defective heart still beats for.
And the tsunami that shreds everything in its path, including the fragile threads holding my barely stitched-together heart.

Note: This novella is a 32,000-word prequel to **In Plain Sight**, Book 4 in the ***Sin and Sinuosity*** series. It ends on a cliffhanger, and the story continues in **In Plain Sight**.

AUTHOR'S NOTE

The events of **Promise Me Forever** pick up approximately six months after **Taste Of Hell** and **Touch Of Heaven** ends.

For an optimal reading experience, reading the first three books in the series (**Taste Of Hell**, **Touch Of Heaven**, and **Six Feet Under**) is suggested.

CONTENTS

Previously On	1
Prologue	7
1. Delilah	9
2. Delilah	14
3. Marc	22
4. Marc	28
5. Delilah	33
6. Delilah	40
7. Harris	46
8. Marc	53
9. Delilah	57
10. Delilah	62
11. Marc	67
12. Marc	75
13. Marc	85
Epilogue	87
Thank You!	94
Acknowledgments	96
Books By Elice Nange	98
About the Author	99
Afterword	100

DELILAH

"What do you think that's about?" David asks.

Harris and I flank David on either side, each of us vying for the baby, but he won't relinquish him. He's in full overprotective dad mode, this one. Although as he cradles Harold, rocking his sleepy figure from side to side, his eyes remain fixated on my sister, who is having a chat with Marc. A scolding, more like, but Dahlia can hold her own.

It is somewhat comforting to know that I wasn't entirely wrong about him the first time. He really is whipped. Completely, utterly in love with her.

"With Marc, it could be anything," Harris says.

"Call it what it is, an olive branch," I chime in.

Then Marc's fingers curl around Dahlia's elbow and she goes completely still. A feral growl erupts from David's chest, causing Harold to wince.

"She's fine," I assure him.

"What the fuck is wrong with him?" David growls. "He knows she doesn't like to be touched. The fucker probably did that on purpose."

Harris snickers; I do too.

What can I say? Whipped.

"No, he didn't," Harris points out. "Look."

We all watch as Marc's hand falls to his side and he watches Dahlia. A few beats pass, and when she opens her eyes, he… apologizes?

We are all at a safe-ish distance from them, and I don't read lips either, but it looked like he just said *'I'm sorry'* or something along those lines.

Progress, right?

"I take it congratulations are in order," David suddenly says.

My stomach flips painfully.

"What?" Harris chokes.

He tears his eyes away from Dahlia, reluctantly, I might add, and his gaze meets Harris's. "The rings. All three of you are wearing matching rings. Did you get engaged or something?"

"You can say that," Harris says. "I suppose the correct term would be a domestic partnership. Or brother husbands."

"Brother husbands?" David asks incredulously.

Harris snickers at his own joke. "It's a thing."

"But Marc isn't your brother," David counters.

"It's not literal." He holds out both arms. "Give me the baby."

"No." David turns his back on him. "Make your own."

"We're working on it, but I need the practice."

"Practice?"

His eyes meet mine, then his gaze lowers, lingering on my stomach, before slowly rising, lingering again on my chest, then my cheekbones, and finally meeting my eyes.

His lips part and I shake my head, mouthing a *'Don't'* to him.

I'm not hiding it, but I'm not exactly celebrating it either. Not yet, anyway. I'm late, that's as far as I know. Everything else will come after, and that's when I'll know for sure. There's no need to get my hopes up now with a test. Not when it will say the same thing it's been saying for months.

Maybe it will be positive this time.

It's what I've always wanted. It's what the guys want too. While Marc will be thrilled, I'm not sure about Harris. If I'm pregnant, there's a ninety percent chance that the baby will be his.

"I still think it's bullshit that you can't legally marry more than one person in Minnesota. Delilah refuses to pick one of us, so—"

"When did this become about me?" I interject.

"Isn't it always? We told you we don't care which of us you commit to, just as long as you do."

"Fine." I huff. "Then you won't care if I married Marc *and* took his last name."

"I… there's no need to go quite that far."

"So I should marry you and take *your* last name?"

"What about Marc?"

"My point exactly."

"Can't it be either-or? Marry one, take the other's last name?"

"I happen to like my last name."

"But you just said—"

"I know what I said. You know, maybe you should try taking my last name. Just a thought."

David snickers, having turned his gaze back to Dahlia. "You already bicker like an old married couple. Why bother with all the fanfare?"

Harris wrinkles his nose. "I dislike fanfare. And drama. And people and their fragile feelings to cater to. I still want a commitment ceremony though."

"You hate parties," I point out.

"Big parties. I'm thinking of a small ceremony with just friends and family. Something that makes this official."

"David and Dahlia don't plan on getting married. It doesn't make them any less committed than they already are."

"Why are you bringing me into this?" David complains.

"Because you're right here, hogging the baby," Harris says. "But since you asked, when do you plan on making an honest woman out of her?"

David and I both snort at the same time.

"An honest woman?" David laughs. "What is this, the Dark Ages? Dahlia will chop off my left testicle if I mention marriage. And this one here," he angles a chin in my direction, "won't hesitate to hold me down while she carves them right out."

I nod. "That's right, I will."

No point in refuting. I am handy with a scalpel. He did break my sister once, so it's his job to make sure that it never happens again, or the repercussions will be severe.

"You could at least pretend not to be enjoying this," he says about the sinister smirk that crosses my face. "And I happen to like my balls right where they are."

"Chicken," Harris teases.

"I can live with that, as long as I get to keep her and this little guy." He presses a kiss to Harold's forehead. "Besides, if anyone's going to be proposing, it'll be Dahlia proposing to me and not the other way around."

"Good luck with that." I tap on his shoulder patronizingly.

"I won't need luck. I'll just charm her pants right off."

"Dude, you already do that," Harris points out.

"I'll just turn it up a thousand more notches then."

They continue talking, and we all continue to not-so-subtly watch Marc and Dahlia like the creeps we all are. Because those two are like oil and water; the whole point of this fucking gathering was for them to make peace with each other. Harris came around fairly quickly, especially when he discovered Dahlia's other issues. And also why it was that she stayed with Curtis all this time. It really was to protect me.

Once David convinced Dahlia to keep the baby, it sealed the deal for him. Watching him like this, I'd say David has really come into his own. He loves Dahlia, and since Harold is hers, he loves him too. It is that simple for him.

He makes it so hard for me to hate him.

Marc, on the other hand, is taking a long time to come around. Too long, if you ask me.

Then Dahlia hands a bottle of breastmilk to Marc, and David growls again.

"Dude, would you fucking chill?" Harris laughs. "Marc is an asshole, but he's not that big of an asshole. Taking food away from a baby is one of the worst cardinal sins in his book."

That seems to appease David some. But when Marc smiles at Dahlia, I'm sure he has steam coming out of both ears.

"Is he trying to charm my girl?" he says.

Harris doubles over in laughter. "Oh man, you really are whipped."

David pouts. "He is! He's really doing it, turning the famous Sotelo charm on her. Don't pretend you don't know it. It's how that fucker got his hooks into you two. Besides, I'm the only one who—"

"That's it. Hand over my nephew and go to her," I order.

Playing the aunt card always works in my favor, but I only use it for special occasions like this one. It works too, since David doesn't protest. He just hands Harold to me and stalks to where she is. Marc approaches us with a serene smile; the usual tightness in his jaw is gone. He's also holding a bottle of Dahlia's breast milk like it ranks in the world's top ten most precious things.

Progress, like I thought.

Also, I need something from him.

———

"You haven't stopped smiling, so it went well," I tell Marc as we all walk out of Charlie's nursery where Harold is settled for his nap.

It's been twenty minutes and the serene look on his face hasn't faded. I'm hoping this is a good sign because I need something from him. Not a book thing, but it comes pretty darn close.

"We agreed to be cordial," he tells us as we head for our bedroom.

David and Dahlia are still on the second floor, since they need a moment to themselves. We do too. Or I do, and I can't ask Marc what I need in front of them.

"Cordial, huh?" I test out the word; it feels clinical. "Did Daa say that, or did you?"

"She did. I just went along with it."

"Yeah right. You didn't just go along with it. You turned on the Sotelo charm, and David was very bothered by it. Did you do that on purpose?"

Not that I care, this works perfectly in my favor.

Harris frowns like he just remembers something. "What did he mean by that?"

Oh boy.

I turn to Marc for help and he lifts both hands in mock surrender, the smile on his face morphing into a smirk. So I turn back to Harris and give him a sweet smile. "What did *who* mean by *what*?"

"David."

I steel myself. "He said a lot of things, Harris. You need to be more specific."

He huffs. "He said, *'I guess congratulations are in order'*, and I know he wasn't referring to the rings."

"It's just a figure of speech," I tell him. "Don't go reading into things."

"Figure of speech my ass. If there's something you're not telling us—"

"Like the fact that D's pregnant?" Marc chooses that moment to chime in, oh so helpfully.

"Who says I'm pregnant?" I answer my own question by wrapping my arms around my stomach. It's a reflex, I swear.

Harris's gaze drops to my stomach, and a look I can only describe as pure elation comes over his face. It will only make this sting like a bitch when the test comes back negative.

"I am not pregnant," I take a step back from him and whip my face to Marc's. "Take it back, Marc."

He shrugs. "Well, there's only one way to find out."

I take another step back. "I am not peeing on a stick while you two clowns watch."

"We can close our eyes if that makes you feel better," Harris adds.

"I don't think so," I say before I sprint towards our bedroom, knowing they will be close behind. Maybe I'll barricade myself in our bathroom before they make it.

It's just my luck that it doesn't happen.

PROLOGUE

DELILAH

Simone said she would never leave me.

Granted, she didn't use those exact words, but it was implied.

She not only implied it, she guaranteed it by asking me to marry her.

Seems silly, doesn't it?

Holding on to words spoken in the heat of the moment. Clinging to promises made when we were both riding out our oxytocin and dopamine highs.

To me, it wasn't just words. It was everything they stood for, everything they meant to me — to us.

She didn't *just* ask me to marry her; she promised me forever. She promised we would have a life together, a home filled with joy and laughter, with lots of babies, and everything I ever wanted.

When you are born defective, like me, you learn not to want for things. You learn that things like hopes, dreams, and wishes are trivial and hold little meaning. I didn't put much stock in those things anyway. Living and surviving from day to day was enough for me.

Until *she* happened.

Until she promised me forever, and in the same breath, she promised me the world. Or rather, that it would be us against the world.

If I wished for it, then it would all be mine. *She* would be mine, forever and always.

I should have known better than to wish for the impossible, but I was also young and naive, so I said yes. I said yes to everything she had to offer, and then some.

Why wouldn't I?

She was my world — *is* my world.

She's my everything, my reason for living, for breathing.

For existing.

I belong to her in every sense of the word; this made things official.

Little did I know, it was all a lie.

Empty promises she made, knowing full well she had no intention of following through on them.

Why promise me forever, only to leave?

Last time I checked, forever doesn't entail ripping my defective heart right out of my chest. Forever doesn't mean leaving me, a shadow of my former self, behind to pick up the pieces. Forever shouldn't imply leaving me alone to forge ahead in a world without her.

If any of that was in the fine print, I must have missed that.

The problem with loving someone is you can't walk away from them and hold on at the same time. You'll break yourself.

I would know.

1

DELILAH

If this is what I get for being kinky, for taking the initiative, and for the absurd lengths I'm willing to go to to keep one man happy, then I'm doing it all wrong.

In the dimly lit basement workshop, the air is heavy with the smell of sawdust and oil and the slick sounds of Harris's and my lovemaking. Out of all the surfaces in this space, I have no idea how we ended up on the floor.

Although the space is surprisingly tidy, considering how much time he spends down here, lost in his creations. But even in its apparent neatness, the workshop exudes raw and untamed sexual energy, a testament to the passion that often consumes him.

Just as *she* consumes me.

The concrete floor beneath my kneecaps is cold and unforgiving, a stark contrast to the heat rising in the space between us.

When we make love, Harris always asks to see everything, all of me, and I give him that. I want to make him happy, even though someone like me, broken and defective, is least deserving of it.

The last thing I'm expecting is for my mouth to betray me, even though I know not even his ministrations to my body can stop the trainwreck that is my lips. My soulmate's name spills past them as Harris rolls his hips, hitting deep within me the sensitive spot that makes my body tremble. It's hard work keeping my eyes open as his cock mercilessly drills into me.

I show him everything, but it's not enough for him.

Nothing ever is.

All that effort on my part to keep things interesting between us, yet all it takes is one little snafu, and we're back to square one. It was a slip of the tongue, and his movements stilled, and then he pulled back slightly from me. "What the fuck did you just say?"

"Nothing," I rush to add, but it's too late.

Nor is it the type of thing one can take back.

In his defense, I accosted him this time, not the other way around.

A few weeks back, Harris shared an elaborate fantasy he's entertained for years, which involved eating me out on his workshop table. That's all I had in mind when I came down here at the crack of dawn and spread myself out on his table like a delectable feast I knew he couldn't resist. Then one thing led to another, and here we are.

The lust in his eyes dissipates a little as they search mine in earnest. "What's it going to take, Delilah?"

My lips part in response, but no sound comes out. The question hangs between us, pregnant with frustration. As the silence stretches thin, an unspoken plea for understanding lingers in the air. It makes the room feel smaller, suffocating almost, as if the weight of our unresolved argument draws the walls nearer, closing in on us.

I bite down on my lower lip, and my gaze travels downwards. *It's just the frustration speaking*, I remind myself as I pull his hand off my ass cheek and place the flat of his palm over my heart.

"This, here," I say, pressing his palm in. "I made you a promise, and I don't intend on going back on my word."

I promised them forever. At no point did I claim said forever didn't also include her.

Harris's eyes look tortured. Pained, even, as he sucks in a resigned breath. His other hand scales up my spine and rests on the back of my head. "You called me by her name," he continues, his voice strained. "You're calling me by her name while I'm buried deep inside you. It's like you're not even trying anymore."

A chill seeps into my bones at his words, and not even the added endorphins swimming through my body are enough to shake this impending feeling of doom that threatens to overtake me.

To combat that feeling, I must stop bothering with the niceties. Nothing I do or say will ever be enough for him. I can jump through all the fucking hoops to satisfy him, but since I can't even fuck him without slipping up, why bother?

Happiness is overrated.

It's so fucking overrated.

I don't know why everyone keeps saying it's the end-all-be-all. It isn't.

Everything he's saying is white noise, but it's the pain in his eyes, so deep and guttural, that completely guts me. I can't bear to look anymore, so I squeeze my eyes shut, his words bruising my already broken heart even more.

"Not now," I force out the words.

What bitchy Delilah wants to say is, *You too, huh? Congratulations. You finally showed your true feelings. It took you fucking long enough.*

Only, she's steering the fucking ship, so she says those things to him anyway.

Harris blows out a breath. "Don't be like that."

"Like what?" I hiss-whisper, irritation seeping in. "I'm fucking horny, and I don't want to talk about it."

"Too fucking bad, Delilah. I do."

Fine. We really are doing this. In that case…

"I don't know why you're acting like this. This isn't new, Harris. You've known me for ages, so you know I can't turn it off. I don't know how to."

And even if I *did* know how to turn it off, I don't want to. I can't. Not when every cell in my body constantly reaches out for Simone, yearning for her. Calling out for her.

My anchor.

My soulmate.

Harris's jaw clenches as if trying to contain the barely contained torrent of conflicting emotions running through him. "Can you at least try?"

Try?

I don't think he understands.

But more importantly, I don't think he fully grasps what she is to me. *Who* she is to me.

And I am so, so fucking of having to constantly explain myself to him, or tiptoe around his fucking fragile feelings on this.

Marc gets it. Why can't he?

Some people are destined for love, while some are destined for pain.

For some, it's a tenuous medium between the two.

Others, like me, are destined to spend the rest of our lives barricaded from what we want.

My eyes spring open, and I gulp down on the nausea threatening to overtake me. This has to be said. It *needs* to be said, consequences be damned. "I can't do this anymore."

His eyes go wide with hurt and disbelief. "What do you mean?"

"This. Us. This constant tug of war. I'm tired of it."

His gaze softens, and the armor around him cracks with vulnerability. "I love you, Delilah. I don't want to lose you."

"That's the fucking problem," I toss back, the desperation in my voice mirroring the turmoil in my heart. "I'm here with you, Harris. We're in this together, all of us. Commitment. Forever. The whole gambit, I'm in. I'm not going anywhere. So why do you keep looking at me like I'm going to bolt at any time? Are you secretly hoping I would, so you can say I told you so?"

A fragile pause hangs between us, a delicate bridge waiting to be crossed or shattered. The choice lingers in the air, a silent invitation for compromise, for understanding.

"For years, I've been trying to understand you, to make sense of what goes on in that gorgeous brain of yours. I have you figured out, for the most part. But this—"

"Isn't a competition," I cut him off, my tone edged with anger and desperation. "Not once did I lie or misrepresent myself to you. This is who I am, and I've been honest with you *both* on this from the beginning. You're not the center of my universe, Harris. You never were, and you never will be. I refuse to let her go…" I hesitate before forcing the words out, knowing how deeply they will hurt him. "Not even for you."

He stares at me as if waiting for me to take it back, but I don't.

I won't.

Instead, my movements are slow and deliberate as I inch back slowly, his still-hard cock slipping out of my weeping cunt. Then I climb off his lap, stand, and retrieve my clothing. "If you don't wanna fuck me anymore, just fucking say so. I'm not gonna beg you to."

In the corner of my eye, I notice he rears back like my words somehow offend him. "That's not the same thing, and you know it."

The sounds of the deadbolts sliding out of place drown out his response. He doesn't need that many fucking locks on the inside door of his workshop, not when I now have free rein to this room, and Marc can get in any time he wants using his secret passageways.

Although, I suspect my privileges will be revoked after this.

What-the-fuck-ever.

It doesn't fucking matter.

I mean every word I just said, even if my lips say one thing and my heart screams another.

How can I take a chance on this, on them, on forever, when I know the pain of loss all too well? How do I move on with them when the ghosts of my past hold me hostage, haunting the present?

I'm halfway up the stairs before calling over my shoulder, "I hear Marc in the kitchen. I'll ask him to come down and finish you off."

See, I'm not a complete bitch. I even infused the right amount of sweetness into my tone — the kind that screams equal parts *Fuck you* and *Bless you.*

The message gets lost in translation because I hear Harris's footsteps behind me. I move faster, refusing to slow down, not even as he repeatedly chants different variations of "Delilah, please, I didn't mean it like that," at my back.

It's not like that changes anything. I know that I fucked this one up, and I don't have it in me to give him a half-assed apology for it. I'd rather be left alone.

My wish is granted as we brush past Marc in the first-floor kitchen. Always so perceptive, he takes one look at us and grabs hold of a protesting Harris, leaving me free to my own devices.

2

DELILAH

The water pelts down upon me, a torrential rain within these four walls. It drowns out the sounds of Harris's and Marc's lovemaking in the next room.

Some days I like to watch them. Other days, like today, I can't bring myself to, not with Harris's words playing on repeat in my mind.

What's it going to take, Delilah?

The fucking impossible, it would seem.

I lean against the cool tiles, their chill seeping through my skin, mirroring the numbness in my heart. The steam cloaks the room, a veil between me and the world outside.

People claim that time heals all wounds. They claim a lot of things, too, but they haven't been subjected to a literal bonfire as a punitive means of getting closure.

I close my eyes, and my body shudders at the memory. Tears intermingle with droplets, tracing a path down my cheeks as I stand beneath the punishing cascade. I can't stop them, no matter how hard I try. If I'm being honest, I'm not so sure I want to stop them.

On days like these, I feel too much of her. In others, it blends into a sea of endless nothingness.

They tell me to let her go. That my soulmate is dead, and I need to move on.

And I *sort of* did, with Marc and Harris.

They want to take things a step further. They want that elusive forever with me and won't back down.

The last time they proposed — the thirty-ninth time, I might add — I caved and finally said yes. I'll never forget the look on their faces. It was a dead-ringer for hers on the night she proposed.

Funny, for nineteen years, I've had one fiancée. Now, I have three.

The shower door slides open, and steam escapes.

"D?"

The words tumble out of me in a rush. "I'm fine. I just needed to be alone for a bit."

In a few strides, Marc closes the distance between us. He presses his body and his rock-hard erection into my thigh. One hand snakes around my lower back, the other cupping my jaw, and he presses his forehead against mine. Our breaths commingle, settling into a familiar rhythm.

His face is only inches from mine as he whispers, "Things would be so much easier if you'd just say the words already."

My lip curls in a half-smile that doesn't quite reach my eyes. "Is that why you followed me in here?"

His eyes flicker with emotion as he considers the question. "No," he breathes. "As it turns out, keeping my hands off you is damn near impossible. You have no idea what you do to me."

I should be happy. I *am* happy.

I'm so fucking happy, it hurts.

Everything hurts.

Every breath I take hurts. And with each passing day, it hurts even more.

I can't shake this bittersweet ache either. It has settled deep within my bones, a cruel reminder of everything and everyone I've loved and lost.

People I love die, or they leave me.

Dr. Goodman. My parents.

Simone.

She and I are connected in a way I could never truly explain. That's why it hurt so much when she left. It feels like I lost a part of my soul that day. I don't just miss her; she's missing from me. How does one move past that?

The sad part is, they know.

Marc and Harris, they've always known.

And I know it isn't fair to them — me using them as substitutes for her — but I can't help it. Nor can I help the words that slip past my lips, words born from a place of selfishness.

"Do whatever you want with me. I'm yours."

Marc pauses, then leans back. He studies me intently, but his stormy gray eyes are drained. Expressionless. Then he pushes off me and takes a step back.

Panic seizes me. This isn't the end, but it certainly feels like one, and I can't have that. "Marc?"

His shoulders slump as he walks to the opposite end of the shower. "I never should have brought you into this."

What?

"This was all a mistake," he adds.

"Why would you say that?" I sigh, overwhelmed with emotion.

I'm too sad to be angry. Too angry to be sad. Too numb to cry.

He pulls at his hair, his gaze downcast. "Isn't it obvious? Because this was—"

"Marc, please," I spit out, exasperated. "I propositioned you both. I moved in with you both of my own accord. I'm here. What more can I do to prove I'm in this for the long haul?"

"At the risk of sounding like H—"

"Don't," I force out, my throat hoarse. "You promised."

His chest heaves. "I would never ask you to give her up."

"You were just about to."

"No. I was going to say, about expanding our family—"

"I haven't changed my mind," I add, cutting him off a second time. "I want a baby. I *need* a baby."

"Even if it kills you?"

I nod. "Even if."

Hesitation flashes in his eyes, yet I can sense the warring conflict dying inside us both.

His lips part to voice the question, and I shake my head.

"Don't," I breathe. "Just… make it hurt. Make me bleed."

In three strides, he closes the distance between us. His hand circles my throat, and forcing my eyes to meet his. Stormy gray eyes search mine as his breath mingles with my own. His fingers dig into the flesh of my throat, but it's not meant to hurt me.

He's possessing me, like I asked. It's what he does — this uncanny ability of his.

Drawing in a shuttered breath, I soften my body, surrendering to him.

This is what I need.

This is what I crave.

I love his possessive side. I love his dark side, too.

He shifts his hips against me, and I let out a breathy moan.

"You're not helping," he warns, his deep voice rumbling through me.

"Was I supposed to?"

In one smooth motion, he flips my body around and flattens me against the bathroom wall. The air leaves me in a swoosh from the surprise and impact. He gets a hold of my wrists and forces them above my head, pinning them in place.

His smooth olive skin, the muscles in his chest, all of him, presses against me. He's so close that I can feel every intake of breath, every erratic beat of his heart, and the bulge between his legs presses against the crack in my ass, letting me know his desires mirror my own.

I want to beg him to fuck me, but all I can do is gasp.

Using his free hand, he trails his fingers down and under my body, between my legs, and cups me. His erection throbs beside my tight pucker in promise.

I close my eyes, and a familiar numbness spreads through me. I want to stay in that place.

Except, he doesn't let me. Not this time.

Instead, I feel light strokes on my neck, my arms, and my back. His cock pulses hot against my thigh, but he doesn't try to put it inside me, not in my weepy cunt or my ass. His hands on me don't even feel sexual. All he does is pet me, and I arch into his caresses.

"Why did you stop?" I mean for it to come out demanding, but instead, I sound weak.

Desperate. Needy.

"I want you here with me," he murmurs against my ear. "I need you in this with me. No hiding in your mind. No tuning me out."

"I wasn't t—"

"I know you weren't, D. Not on purpose. The thing is, as long as we are together, there is no hiding. Not from each other. Not like this."

That's not what Harris said, I want to add, the words stuck in my throat.

He turns me to face him, then presses his lips to mine and forces his tongue into my mouth. His hands stay on my breasts, massaging the tender and sensitive flesh. He kneads my nipples between his fingers, stroking them, tweaking them as he rolls the sensitive nub between both fingers.

It's odd, but I can feel the difference between his touch now, compared to before. Now, he's not trying to punish me any longer. He wants to play with me for his own pleasure. And in a way, it's what I need too. It's uncanny how well he understands what I need, even without me saying the words out loud. He understands that sometimes I need to disappear into my own head, and he gives me that. Just as long as I'm not using intimacy as an escape but rather as a means of bonding.

"Do you trust me?" he whispers.

It's a simple enough question, but something twists up inside of me. "Always."

He lifts me and carries me into the bedroom. Our other half is nowhere to be found.

"Where's Harris?" I can't help but ask, my voice hoarse.

His full lips tremble for the barest second. "He hightailed it to his basement workshop."

Avoiding me, no doubt. Still, he got what he wanted from Marc, then just left him hanging?

Typical.

Marc's chest heaves, and his Adam's apple bobs as he swallows. "Should I get him?"

I shake my head. "I just need you."

My mind might be blanking out, but my body's a pool of liquid heat.

"What did you and H fight about?" His question catches me off guard.

My lust dissipates a little. "I don't want to talk about it."

It's not that hard to put two and two together. Harris being sulky, me crying in the shower, and Marc playing referee between us. There could be a million reasons for it, but he's fucking smart and will narrow it down.

Marc places me on the bed and climbs in after me before pulling me on top of him, so I'm straddling his hips with my legs on either side of him, resting my hands on his chest. His arousal bobs up towards my hanging breasts.

His cock looks dark and thick and wet at the tip. Something softens in a deep, cold place inside my chest. But when my hand trailed downwards, my intentions clear, he stopped me by placing his hand on mine. Our eyes meet, mine stunned, but he gives me a slight shake of his head.

"Do you trust me?" he asks again.

It's not like him to seek validation from me. Twice.

Still, I give it to him anyway.

"I do. I also need you, Marc. I need to feel you."

For a brief moment, he looks conflicted. I'm not sure why, as he's the one who brought us in here. He could've given me a quick fuck in the shower, but he chose to prolong this by bringing us in here, to our bed specifically. There's never anything quick or hurried about our lovemaking.

He maneuvers my hips onto his erection, then down, slowly. The tautness of his face speaks to the urgency of the situation, but he holds my hips still, giving my body a moment to get used to the feeling of being full, of being so utterly consumed by him.

Once we've centered ourselves in the moment, with our gazes locked on each other; only then does he begin to move. He rocks up with tiny thrusts. Slow, languid thrusts as he hits that tender spot deep inside of me over and over again. It takes me a beat, but my body catches the rhythm and blends right into it. Once he's satisfied as I match his thrusts, he releases my hips and smooths one hand back along my ass. The other hand moves to my breasts, stroking them, tweaking them as he did in the bathroom earlier.

"Was it her?" he murmurs, his stormy gray eyes locked onto mine.

I'm certain I don't want to discuss my fucked-up-ness with him, not right now. So I lean into his touch, and he sucks my nipple into his mouth.

My arousal builds, taunting me, and my movements speed up.

Marc's hand tightens on my ass, as if to say *No, not yet.*

Fair enough.

No more hiding.

My body relaxes into the rocking motion as the pleasure between my legs grows.

This part is new to us. This slow, languid lovemaking type feels more like a dance or meditation. It's the type of fucking I do with Harris, not Marc. With Marc, I can count on pain. With Harris, it's

all about the connection. Flipping things around like this, it's…
different.

Yet, it shouldn't surprise me.

As they both claim, ever since we stumbled into each other's lives,
Marc has been discovering many things not just about himself, but
about me. About Dahlia too, but he keeps saying cryptic shit — things
like how alike they are, how perfect they are for each other.

Which, in turn, is giving her all sorts of crazy ideas that she'd like
to run my him. By Marc, I mean.

But, I digress.

I have no idea how much time passes as we're like this. Him
sucking down on my nipples, alternating between the buds. My fingers
dig into the hard planes of his stomach, probably leaving gashes
behind. This doesn't deter him. If anything, it prompts him to slow
down his thrusts even further. Until my legs grow sore and tingly, and
my own thrusts slow.

He rolls us over and surges into me deeper, in an aggressive rhythm
that takes me faster and harder. I pull my legs higher and curl my hands
lightly on his neck, opening my body in supplication. I wasn't an active
participant any longer. I couldn't help him or even react — I can only
take it.

My orgasm sneaks up on me and I come again, only this time it
wasn't in a blinding explosion but a soft wave. Not a crest but a low
thrum of pleasure, each tender wave accented with each of his thrusts.

Her name hovers on the tip of my tongue, threatening to spill out,
so I clamp down on my bottom lip hard enough for the coppery tinge to
flood my senses.

Harris was right about one thing. The only time I'm truthful with
them is when their cocks are buried inside me so deep that I can't see
straight. Now's not the time for that. I already hurt Harris. I can't afford
to alienate Marc, too.

Marc buries his face into the side of my neck, groaning roughly as
he comes. His whole body rumbles at the sound, shuddering at his
release. His arms tighten their hold on my body, and his hips push
down into me, harder, deeper. My eyes are squeezed shut when his
thrusts slow; then I feel his thumb pulling down my lip harshly before
his mouth covers mine, kissing away the sting.

He's drinking me in, consuming me just as she does to me.

"I love you," he whispers against my swollen lips, then his warm palm cups my cheek, wiping away my tears with his thumb. I thought I was all cried out, but these ones sneaked up on me. They were tears I wanted to hide, a deep-seated grief for what could've been. Still, I lean into his touch as he thumbs away at the wetness that flows as I cry quietly for who knows how long.

Eventually, my eyelids flutter, then open, to find his stormy orbs fixated on mine.

The words spill out before I can rein them in.

"I think I lost the baby."

3
____

MARC

"Marc, can I talk to you for a second?" Dahlia asks the following Friday, after our standing monthly attorney-client meeting.

She also spent the last ten minutes of our meeting pacing the room, and I was curious about that.

Instead of asking, I glance at Delilah, who shrugs as she rises.

"Good luck," is all she says before walking out, leaving me alone with her sister.

Okay then.

"What is it?"

"It's about David."

"What about him?"

She shifts on her feet. "I… this is embarrassing."

No shit.

I lean back in my seat and fold my arms over my chest. "Try the other side of this conversation," I force out. "It's awkward as hell."

It's barely been a week since we agreed to be cordial with each other. We even called a fucking truce. Neither of us is quite comfortable in our new normal now, so this should be interesting.

Dahlia walks over to where I'm seated, pulls out another chair, and places it directly before me. She sits and leans forward with fingers steepled together.

"It's about our sex life." She opens with that, dropping the bomb on me. "David's and mine."

I blink once, then twice.

What the actual fuck?

"What makes you think I'd even entertain this conversation?"

She flinches but stands her ground. "That's fair. I get it. We've had our differences, and we're never going to see eye to eye on many things. And that's okay. This is a humiliating request for me to make, but I'm doing it anyway. Because I love him and because I would do anything for him. I would do anything to make him happy because his happiness is just as important to me as my son's and Dee's. And also, I'm coming to you, not Harris, because I know you've always had a soft spot for him."

Where was this fucking backbone when the McWhorters walked all over her for twenty years?

I lean forward, mirroring her stance. "All right, I'm listening."

She draws a deep breath and releases it slowly. "David needs… more."

"Define more."

I know what she's asking me, but I prefer her to spell it the fuck out for me.

I'm nice like that.

She shifts in her seat, even as she looks me directly in the eye. "He needs more, sexually. More than I can give him. I know he loves me, and I love him too. But sexually, I also know that I'm not enough for him."

My lip quirks ever so slightly upwards. "Does David know that you're having this conversation with me?"

"What do you think?"

"He would be pissed that you're even considering pimping him out. Again."

I mean, seriously? We barely put the whole Nalina debacle behind us.

She runs a hand over her face. "I considered that possibility too, yes. That's why I'm here, talking to you instead of Harris. David told me about the sex contracts. How they came about. He said it was your idea to do them in the first place. And that you refused to touch him without having one in place."

That fucker and his big mouth.

"I realize it now; they were meant to protect him," she continues. "Not just his assets, but also his heart."

"I am his attorney. It's my job to have his best interests at heart."

"Yeah, but you put those in place long before you became his attorney. And I also know that despite what he says, it was your idea to break things off in the first place. Did you tell him the reason why?"

"He's my client. I don't fuck my clients."

"Bullshit," she counters. "Dee is your client, and you fuck her. You wanted to fuck her fifteen years ago before she became your client. You almost fucked her seven years ago, and she was your client then too. Tell me, how is David any different?"

My jaw clenches.

Fucking Hurricane Dahlia.

Why am I entertaining this conversation again?

That's right. Mom taught me to always leverage relationships to my advantage. Do unto others, or it will be done to you.

Somehow that doesn't seem to be the case here.

But, as it so happens, there is something that I need from her.

"D is different, and I don't have to explain myself to you."

"Be that as it may, you should have explained yourself to David then. You should have told him the real reason you ended things, not this bullshit story about attorney-client boundaries."

"And what's the real reason?"

"You love him," she deadpans. "You and Harris, you both love him."

"I think you are reading into things a little too much."

"I'm only stating the obvious. You had an open relationship for years and never kept any of your other partners around after things ended. Yet you keep him around. I know it was never about money. I also know it's not out of the goodness of your hearts. There's a lot more to this big brother mentor-mentee protégé relationship that you three keep going on and on about. Your connection has always been as sexual as it is physical and emotional. Official or not, he is as much a part of your family as you are his. You all know his daughter, which is outside the usual attorney-client parameters.

"David loves you both in his own twisted way, even though he will never admit it. Since you all were too chicken to admit it back then, I'll say it now. None of you were ready to let him go back then, so you all found other ways to keep each other around and skirted around the real issue. But I know the real reason you broke things off."

"Are you always this long-winded?"

Her golden brown eyes narrow in annoyance. "It's because Dee didn't like it."

I swear, these two sisters will be the death of me. Is there some rule that states twins must tell each other everything?

"That had nothing to do with—"

"It's why Harris started that stupid game in the first place. It was for her. It's why you went along with it too. It was all for her. And had Dee been okay with it, your thing with David would have gone on for longer than the year it was. But since you are perceptive, you picked up on her displeasure and broke things off with him. I get it, though. You made the best decision you could for your family, and ultimately you chose Dee over him. I can't fault you for that. I really can't. David was young and needed time to grow, become more comfortable with himself and his sexuality, stand on his own, and go after what he wanted all by himself. I'd say it was a blessing in disguise. I'm so fucking glad that's how the cookie crumbled because he met me.

"That said, I also know you weren't a fan when he returned to Nalina afterward. You knew what she was doing to him, so you did what you could to protect him. The contracts. The vetting. Other things he knew about but chose to look the other way. I'm sure you did much more that he doesn't know about. Still, it was always up to him to walk away, and you let him know that in your own way. But he didn't because she provided him with something he needed — lots and lots of it.

"That was my biggest fear, you know? That she sunk her claws so deep into him that he wouldn't be able to cut that fucking cord on his own. She had him for so long and I didn't feel I could compete with what they had. I don't want to touch the other thing since we don't need to rehash that baggage. But know that I took a fucking chance when I ended things with him because I needed him to cut that cord on his own. I'm done with that now, whether you believe me or not."

"The point, Dahlia. Get to it."

"Do you know what gets me about this whole thing? All these people in his life, and no one fucking chose him. That stops. I meant what I said last week. David is my forever, and that's not going to change. And even though he's cut ties with Nalina, it doesn't take away his need. That is why I'm here, setting aside my pride and having this humiliating conversation in the first place. I'm asking if you would reconsider giving him what he needs. Giving him what I can't give him. You are the guy that makes things happen. You are the guy who gives people what they want as well as what they need. And David, he needs this. I don't want to lose him, obviously. But I can't exactly fix what I don't have. This shortcoming of mine."

Shit.

It irks me that I see what David sees in her. It was foolish of me to even question it. I don't anymore since it's the same thing I saw in Delilah from the moment we met.

Loath as I am to admit it, Dahlia is right about everything.

But as it turns out, I'm not the only perceptive one. Delilah already brought me up to speed on most of this. I'm guessing not all of it, though, as Dahlia doesn't realize exactly what she's asking for. But I will spell it out for her since I'm nice like that.

Also, I need something from her, and it is going to be a difficult ask — for her, that is.

"I'll consider it," I tell her. "But on one condition."

"Anything." She purses her lips, then adds, "Just as long as it's within reason."

"Andrea McWhorter."

She frowns. "That is *not* within reason, Marc."

"I know it's not, but the woman insists on talking to you and D together."

"If this is about Curtis's and my custody arrangement, you can tell her to shove it."

"It's not about that." And this custody thing has been a nightmare, with no reprieve in sight. But this ain't it. "Frankly, I'm not sure what this is about, only that it's important. Life or death, she claims."

The woman won't give up until she gets them both in a room with her. The answer has been the same for months. It's also getting to be tedious, maiming her messengers to get the point across. Sadly, that part stopped being enjoyable after the tenth one. Not that she's taken the hint.

"What makes you think I want to be in the same room as that woman, much less breathing the same air she is?"

"You put up with it for twenty years."

"No, I went along with it because it was the path of least resistance. There's a difference. And I don't have to do that anymore. That's why I have you to handle all the legal mumbo jumbo, because I really, *really* don't want to. If not for me, you'll continue to do it for Dee's favorite nephew."

She has me at that.

"Well, there's something to getting closure. I never had that with my mom, as you know. You and D never had that with your parents. Maybe, in a twisted way, this would be the closure that you two need. I can fix it such that this is the last time anyone from that family can ever make such a request from you two."

"And if I do this, you'll reconsider—"

"I don't say shit I don't mean, Dahlia. That applies professionally and personally. Ask your sister. Oh wait, you already know. You two clearly lack any sort of filter."

She pauses and worries her bottom lip. "What makes you think Dee would be interested in anything that woman has to say?"

"I brought this up to her first, obviously. She's thinking along the same lines as you are. You know she loathes that family even more than you do. She will never forgive them after what happened to Simone. But she got out nineteen years ago. She has been out all this time, but you haven't. You had to put up with that the whole time. It's only been a year since you got out, and D is considering that. She refuses to entertain the idea if you won't."

4

———

MARC

It takes her all of two seconds to make up her mind. "I'll do it."

Damn.

Not gonna lie; a small part of me wished she would say no.

She must really, *really* love him.

I'm not one to look a gift horse in the mouth, so I better rope her into this before she thinks it through and backs out of it. "Okay then, I'll arrange it. A week from today. As for this thing with David—"

"Wait a minute." She holds up a hand to me. "You knew I was going to say yes, didn't you?"

I shrug. "Everyone knew except you. You've been busy with the fourth trimester. You love David. All I did was leverage that to make the best of an already shitty situation. D wanted to do it, but she turned it down out of respect for you. David caught wind of it when the requests started coming in, and he was adamant that no one should bring this to your attention. H just wants this over and done with, so he was going to resort to emotional blackmail to get there. All things considered, I am your best option. That shouldn't come as a surprise. I leverage shit all the time. It's what makes me such a good attorney."

Her hand falls and she steeples her fingers together. "Whatever."

"Now, about this thing with David. Nothing happens, not even that initial conversation that all five of us need to have, not unless we are all on the same page about it. We'll get it in writing if that's what it takes. I draw the line at unexpectedly springing this on him. That part is nonnegotiable. So you have to tell him about it ahead of time and in private. That should happen between the two of you. No half-assing it either. I have my ways of checking these things."

"Okay, I can do that."

I know she won't be a fan of this next part. "You know how we operate, yeah?"

She nods. "You share."

"There's that, yes. But that's not all there is to it."

"I'm not doing this for me, Marc. I'm doing this for David."

"Dahlia, the way we operate, sharing goes both ways," I tell her.

Then I give her as long as she needs to let that sink in.

When it does, her eyes widen. "Oh."

Unlacing my fingers, I hold a hand out to her. "Put your hand in here."

She unlaces her fingers and tucks them underneath her thighs. "Oh… umm… do I have to?"

"You don't have to do anything you don't want to," I tell her. "I'm just telling you how it is. That's not how we operated in the past, and it's not how David operated either. It's why we have all these rules in place. It's why those sex contracts existed in the first place."

She swallows thickly. "Can you… can you please explain to me what the rules are?"

Huh.

As far as I can tell, Dahlia is not kinky. All her life, she's only had two sexual partners. It's not a criticism of her preferences, just an observation. Her thixophobia holds her back. I see nothing wrong with that since it takes a lot to trust yourself and your body with another person. Even though she is curious, this is a legit medical condition that will get in the way of what she's asking for.

The thing is, it's bad. I know it's fucking bad. Last weekend, I touched her elbow without warning and she almost had a panic attack. From what D has told me, she's always been this way and it has only gotten worse as she got older, except she's gotten much better at hiding it. Same as she does with her panic attacks.

I find the whole thing to be quite ironic because she does touch people. She touches a lot of people — all the time. As an OBGYN, she cannot *not* touch people. Except it is always non-sexual touches, and she's always the one who initiates the touching. It's how she's gotten around it.

Over the years, there have been rare occasions where I witnessed her subtly cringing when other people touched her. I'm guilty of misreading it at first. At first, I thought she was just being a bitch when she did that until D explained it to me. Then I felt like an idiot and a hypocrite for having misjudged her that way. Especially since, as it turns out, there's a very short list of people whose touch she is okay with — Delilah, David, and baby Harold.

Sexually, that number dwindles down to exactly one.

This will be a shift, and it will not be like riding a fucking bike.

She knows this too; it's why she did this whole thing with David in the first place. Curtis was her first and only for a very long time, until she walked away from her twenty-year relationship on their wedding day. She started out as David's client not long after that, while she was pregnant, and ended up falling in love with him. And yes, I had my reservations about them initially, but I see now that they are legit. David is a different man. A changed man. What they have is real, and I'm glad he has that. I'm happy they have each other.

And she must really love him to be considering this, even with her thixophobia. Since she wants to do this for him, the least I can do is lay it all out for her.

"For the purposes of this conversation, what hat do you want me to wear?"

She blinks. "I don't know what that means."

"Lawyer, sister's boyfriend, cordial friend, or all of the above?"

"Oh." She swallows thickly. "Not lawyer. A combination of the rest."

Smart choice. "There are many rules, but the main one is the sharing component. First, it's up to you and D how you want to handle things between you. But for this to actually work, I have to touch you. We all do, and that includes H. David too. Probably all at once."

Her chest heaves ever so slightly. "I—"

"I hope you know that sugarcoating this won't help. It is what it is when you enter a sexual relationship with multiple people. It's not just about sex; it's also about trust. You say you want this for him, but this isn't just about him. It's about you too. That's something that David knows, and it's probably why he hasn't brought this up to you. So, if you are second-guessing yourself and wondering if you are enough for him, he probably knows it too. Do you understand what I'm saying?"

She nods but doesn't say anything.

"Just as H and I are very protective of D, David is very protective of you. Physically. Emotionally. Sexually. Have you thought about how it would make him feel, seeing you sexually intimate with another man? Even if it's us? And that's if you can actually stomach either of us touching you.

"Flip the coin. David is bisexual. Have you thought about how it would make you feel seeing him sexually intimate with another man? Or with another woman, even if that woman is your sister?"

Her eyelids flutter closed, and her chest heaves. "I-I didn't think about that. About all the nuances that go into it. I thought it was as simple as you all doing your thing while I stayed away."

I can't help the chuckle that bubbles up from within. "There are couples that do that, but it's not that simple either. If you are unfamiliar with the lifestyle, you will only drive yourself crazy by staying away. It won't be any different from what Curtis used to do, and it will hit home a little too close for your comfort. I'm aware he slept with your friends, but the ones who truly cared about you, like Charlena and Leah, knew not to cross that line because they knew how much it would hurt you.

"For the record, that's what Nalina is counting on too. She's counting on *this* being the thing that breaks you two up, and on him coming back to her when shit hits the fan. When that happens, she will be weaseling her way back into your life, restraining order or not. If you go down this path, know that you are opening up your relationship to all these possibilities and outcomes. Good or bad.

"You don't have to answer me, but you and David need to discuss it. It's not the kind of thing you spring on someone in a group setting. Tell him everything you told me today, and also the things you *aren't* telling me. Be prepared for him to get mad. As in, he'll be pissed off at you, and he'll disappear for days. But he will come back to you. I know he will. He could say yes, but he could also say no. If he says no, you might not like it, but you must respect it. And if he says yes, then understand that this is what he is agreeing to. The worst thing either of you can do is go along with it just because it's what the other person wants. So whatever answer or reaction he gives you, make sure you read between the lines and act accordingly."

Her eyelids eventually part and her mesmerizing golden-brown eyes fixate on mine. Eyes identical to the ones I have been staring at for years, but what I see in Dahlia's eyes is something I rarely see.

Vulnerability.

And I just know then that I'm fucked.

That's the problem with these Brewer sisters and their doe eyes. And their… everything else.

"Thank you," she says, "For explaining this to me."

I smile. "Anytime. As for this business with Andrea, I'll let you know when and where this meeting will take place. The sooner we get that over with, the better for all of us."

5

─────────

DELILAH

"You have exactly," I steal a glance at my phone, "ten minutes, so talk fast or we are leaving."

Andrea plasters on one of her signature patronizing smiles. "Girls, after three and a half decades, don't I deserve more than ten minutes of your time?"

Dahlia is seething at this. Not that I blame her, because I am too. I don't think we should be giving this woman any more of our time, but Marc believes we need to hear her out for some reason. He also said we won't like what she has to say, so there's that.

Plus, she seems intent on dragging out whatever this is, and I've just about had it with her. Dahlia beats me to it though.

"If this meeting is a ploy to get me away from my son, you will regret it," she bites.

"It is no such thing," Andrea fake screeches, her poor acting skills on display.

She should know that her shocked face isn't fooling anyone. So I pull my phone out and call up the security feed for the house — our childhood home, the one our parents left Dahlia and me — courtesy of David before he moved in there. He had those installed no more than twenty-four hours after he convinced Dahlia to give him a chance. He is thorough; I'll give him that. He's also obsessed with Dahlia's safety and, by extension, Harold's. If it were anyone else I would be worried, except he's shown time and time again how reliable and resourceful he can be. At least he's putting his skills to good use.

Turning my phone over, I show Andrea the live feed. "Who are these guys? Tourists?"

"How should I know?" Andrea is determined to keep this charade going.

The McWhorters have always been predictable. I count three tinted town cars driving down our street within seconds of each other. Two burly men are circling the perimeter. The idiots probably haven't yet realized they've triggered the perimeter alert at least five different times. Oh well. Once Marc's men get their hands on these idiots, they may think twice about their choice of employer in the future.

"I hope you offer good medical and life insurance to all your employees. They will need it once the Sotelos are done with them."

Dahlia snatches the phone from my hand. "The blonde one is Matthias's right hand. He would never sneeze without your husband's say-so. The other one is new. Another mercenary, a foreign one, I'm guessing? He's in pretty bad shape, Andrea. What hellhole did you pull him out of?"

"I have nothing to do with that," Andrea says. "That's why I'm here. To talk, to clear the air once and for all."

I don't buy it. "You have assassins circling our house. Do you seriously expect us to believe you?"

"I don't control my husband or his actions, despite what you think."

"Still, you knew this was going to happen, yet you arranged this meeting," Dahlia says. "What will happen will happen — hospitalizations, funerals, or whatever else the Sotelos deem necessary to get the message across. Just know that everything that follows from here on out, that's on you."

"Again, none of that is my doing."

"Be that as it may, this is your warning. Call your dogs off. Or better yet, call your husband. Or plan their funerals. Knowing how you operate, there's no doubt you'll find a way to spin their tragic deaths into positive publicity for your family. What do you think will happen when we release this video? What do you think will happen when we release the contracts your in-laws signed with my parents, depicting their so-called good deed that is tantamount to slavery?"

She pulls out her phone and dials. "They know," is all she says before hanging up. "There, happy?"

"Not even close," Dahlia continues. "To think that all this is going on while I have been cordial with your son. We share custody of Harold so that you can be in his life, but Curtis wants nothing to do with his son. That's not my fault. That one's on you and your husband for forcing a child on us. A child that neither of us wanted."

"You seem to be doing just fine," she mumbles sarcastically before adding, "especially with that boy toy of yours."

Dahlia's spine straightens like it always does anytime *anyone* throws a not-so-subtle jab at her relationship with David. "What was that?"

Andrea's gaze darts up and down Dahlia's frame, assessing her body language. "I said, your boy toy certainly keeps things interesting—"

Dahlia's sharp intake of air has the hairs on my arm standing at attention. "Call David a boy toy one more time. I fucking dare you."

Andrea lifts a curious brow, then glances across the room to where the guys are seated. Huddled, more like, and not at all being subtle about the fact that they are listening in on our conversation.

It's one thing for her to demand a sit-down with us, but did she really think the guys would sit this one out?

"My apologies. Your boyfriend," she begrudgingly corrects, "certainly keeps things interesting, playing surrogate daddy. I was under the impression kids weren't his thing."

Dahlia sighs in disbelief, echoing how I'm feeling inside and out. "And yet he's more of a father to Harold than your son is capable of. Not that my personal life is any of your fucking business. It stopped being your fucking business when I walked out on that fucking charade of a wedding. Stick your nose into my personal life, and I will chop it to the stomp. Are we clear?"

A beat passes, and then Andrea mumbles, "Crystal."

Dahlia's shoulders relax a little. "Besides, I'm only doing what I can to make the best of a shitty situation. After everything you did, I should have gone public with this information, but I didn't. You should have left things at that, but that's not enough for you, is it? You want Harold too, and for what? To keep this twisted cycle going?" She shakes her head, letting out a mirthless laugh. "Mercenaries. Honestly, Andrea. Is that any way to treat your precious grandson?"

Andrea's unsophisticated snort is music to my ears. "He's not my precious anything. All I ever wanted was for you to stay as far away from my family as possible."

"Are you serious?" Dahlia asks.

Andrea must think Dahlia and I are still the naive sixteen-year-old girls she once knew and pushed around at will, even going so far as to force them to watch as they burned all of Simone's things.

And now?

She picked an establishment owned by the McWhorters. That sends a clear message across. I'm sure she was under the misguided belief that she was in charge, that we were in her territory and wouldn't be able to fight back should she do something to us. She should have read the room when she came in. I did. All the cameras in here have been disabled, courtesy of David. Half the patrons present are from Marc's security team.

"You know, that's quite rich, coming from you," I eventually say. "Look at where we are."

"I know you don't believe me, and that's your prerogative. Maybe wait until you've heard the whole story before passing judgment. What do you think I've been doing all these years?"

"Playing into your husband's bullshit," Dahlia answers. "You have a minute left."

Her lips press into a fine line. She laces and unlaces her fingers together. Once a minute is up, Dahlia and I both rise, like we rehearsed this ahead of time.

"As fun as this is," Dahlia says, her voice tight, "let's not do it again. Not unless it's inside a courtroom."

"I never should have made that deal with your parents," Andrea quietly says.

That stops us in our tracks. Dahlia and I lock eyes for a second, then she nods, and we sit back down.

"You earned yourself another five minutes," I tell her. "Make it worthwhile."

She nods. "Jordana was my best friend," she starts. "Well, best friend doesn't quite describe what we were to each other. What she was to me. The more accurate representation would be everything."

Dahlia's brow scrunches. "Everything?"

"She was my everything," she clarifies. Her eyes lift to meet Dahlia's. "Like you are to David." She shifts her face to look at me. "Like you are to Harris and Marc." A beat passes, then she adds, "Like you were to Simon." She turns away at that, her gaze downcast. "It was a different time then, obviously. But Jordana was never one to simply go with the flow. She was never one to do things the way they had always been done. She wanted the three of us to run away to Paris and live out our happily ever after together. Paris was as far away as we could get back then without my family finding us. But I was a coward, afraid to go after what I wanted. And also betrothed to Matthias at the time, so running away wasn't an option. His family's resources were considerably more vast, and they had connections across the globe. If we ran, it was only a matter of time before they found us, and the consequences would have been dire."

She leans back and blows out a long, resigned breath. "How I envy you both and your ability to live and love freely." She laughs; the sound is strained and painful. "And yes, I envied Simon too. I envied him for knowing what and whom he wanted. I envied that he was always prepared to fight for it. Consequences be damned."

I have to grit my teeth to keep from correcting her. Dahlia is doing the same thing too. We did promise her five minutes; the least we can do is sit through this poor attempt to rewrite history and this insufferable misuse of Simone's pronouns. Although, it is not all that shocking to learn that Andrea was in love with Mom and Dad and that the feeling was mutual.

Out of all our friends, our parents were the most open-minded. Our friends envied us for the freedoms we had and the liberties we took. But also, it was common knowledge that our parents were the go-to for anyone who needed advice or help. Simone went to them first when she struggled with her identity. Dahlia and I often joked that they wouldn't have been that open-minded to much of what went on under their roof had they not had personal experience with it. All Mom would say was, "'A lady doesn't kiss and tell'".

If I ask that question, how would Andrea answer it?

Instead, we stay silent and let her continue with this sordid tale.

"When my in-laws first had the idea of hand-selecting companions for our children, I should have told them to pound rocks, especially after learning what it would entail. But I didn't, because I naively thought it would be a blessing in disguise for my friends. I know how that sounds, but Jordana and Derrick were struggling, and here I was, pregnant with minimal effort on my part. The thing is, I was pregnant with Simon at the time, and like you," she angles her chin in Dahlia's direction, "I didn't want children either. It was just what was expected of women in my position, and I couldn't refuse to do my part. But Jordana wanted to be a mother so badly, and watching her go through infertility broke my heart. So I talked with them about it before bringing it up to my in-laws. It was the perfect arrangement — my in-laws paid for their fertility treatments and prenatal costs. In return, they were to raise any children born and hand them over once they were of marriageable age.

"As you know, your parents had two late miscarriages and a stillbirth before you two were born. That kind of thing comes with strings attached, and they were intent on getting back every penny spent. Jordana and Derrick were so grateful to finally become parents that they would have agreed to anything my in-laws threw at them.

"By the time you two finally took, I was pregnant with Curtis. You have no idea how happy I was to finally experience this with my best friend. Even so, I had it easy while hers was a high-risk pregnancy with twins. There was always the chance that one or both of you wouldn't make it. But my in-laws were thrilled to learn you were both girls, so they spared no expense. After all, you two were to be married to their grandsons.

"It was my idea that you four be raised together since it was our dream — Jordana's and mine — that our children be best friends like we were. Derrick made the argument for it too. He said that if you all organically fell in love, it would look less like ownership — which my in-laws originally wanted — and be a more genuine relationship. For years that worked just fine, until Simon started off with this craziness—"

I suck in a sharp breath, and Dahlia places a hand over mine. "Your five minutes are up, Andrea. Say anything else stupid and we're walking," she says.

She huffs a breath but continues. "Jordana and Derrick were always better at this parenting thing. Better than I was, far better than I ever imagined. They were naturals with you kids, so it's no surprise you all gravitated to the Brewer house. Which was just fine by me. I wasn't jealous or envious, not when it kept my house clean and orderly. Motherhood was forced on me, and I detested every second of it. You better believe I was too happy to let someone else take it on.

"For the record, I didn't want you girls to end up with my boys, regardless of what the contract said. I told Jordana and Derrick this too, but you kids were inseparable by then. I tried to split you up by sending the boys to boarding school in Europe, but they only lasted a month. So pathetic, all of you. Curtis was always whining about wanting to come home, and you two," she waves a hand between us, "end up hospitalized for who knows what. I had the chance to enjoy a child-free life for the first time in seventeen years, but Derrick couldn't let me have that. Jordana backed him up like she always did. She even took it upon herself to go over my head and straight to my in-laws. Something about wanting healthy, happy children over sick, sad ones. So they brought them back from Europe, and you kids paired yourselves off shortly afterward.

"If you recall, I was vehemently against this. But, as always no one listened to me. You all saw me as the Debbie Downer, the hater of love and happy endings. And since they were the cool, fun parents, obviously, all four of you gravitated to your house. They also let you all do whatever you wanted, so I knew all four of you were sexually active. Again, I was outvoted on that because it's what my in-laws wanted. They bought into the rhetoric that it looked better if you were childhood sweethearts who ended up together instead of the transactional lab rats you were.

"Then Simon started all the nonsense about being born in the wrong body. I still think it was utter nonsense, but I finally saw my chance. The opportunity was golden, if I do say so myself. It was the perfect chance to drive a wedge between you four, and I would have been an idiot not to have taken it. It was no coincidence that you," she angles her chin in Dahlia's direction, "and Simon overheard our conversation that night. After hearing that, I expected him to break things off with Delilah since he claimed to love her so much. And if he didn't, I knew you wouldn't be able to resist telling Delilah what we discussed, and she would be the one to break things off with him. It never occurred to me that Simon would up and leave. Which was just as well because I made sure that even if he did decide to come back, you," she waves a hand in my direction, "wouldn't be all pathetically waiting and pining for him. It is rather unfortunate you turned out the way you were after that, but I regret nothing. It kept you out of my family, did it not?"

6

DELILAH

There's nothing I would love more than to reach into this woman's mouth and rip her tongue out of her head.

But Dahlia keeps me in check as Andrea blabbers on, making sure to issue not-so-subtle reminders that an attack would be ill-advised. Her hand is still on my arm, and she gives it a not-so-gentle squeeze for the third time today, plus a slight shake of her head.

'Don't engage,' she mouths.

But Andrea isn't done. She turns on Dahlia next, pinning her with a pointed glare.

"But you. I never met a bitch incapable of taking a fucking hint until you. You had the perfect out back then; why didn't you take it? Jordana and Derrick certainly did, and as sad as it was to lose my best friend, it also meant they were free of my toxic family. That's something I could live with. But not you, little miss perfect. Even with everything I threw at you, you just stuck around like mold. No one wanted to be stuck with your needy ass for another eighteen years. Not even Curtis, even though he didn't have the guts to tell you so himself.

"I knew what his grandparents were doing to him back then, and I know what his father does to him now. Still, tough shit. If you had left when you should have, he would have grown himself a fucking backbone. He would have been just fine. But you took advantage of that, didn't you? You knew he would never break things off, yet you stayed with him. Then again, you've always been pathetic. No self-respecting woman would have stayed, what with all the cheating. Still, you couldn't take the fucking hint.

"I know what Matthias said to you before you and Curtis got engaged. He told you he would turn Delilah here into a broodmare if you didn't marry my pathetic son. That should have been your fucking cue to run, but you didn't. Not even when I picked an outdoor wedding venue in the spring. Not even when I basically commandeered your entire wedding planning process. Not even when I picked out all of your outfits, down to your fucking underwear. Not even the snafu with your birth control was enough to get you to walk. That was my doing, by the way. As someone who has always been vocal about not wanting children, you had several options for taking care of the problem. Someone like me, who was married off into that family against her will, didn't have that option back then. You can't imagine how frustrating it was for me that you didn't make a beeline for an abortion clinic. Instead, you just had to drag another person into this messed up family."

As she talks, a dull ache starts in my arm and spreads to an unbearable limit. A quick glance tells me the source of said pain is Dahlia's fingernails digging into the sensitive flesh of my arm. It's just as well. I would rather she clawed at my arm than publicly assaulted another woman. We already got into trouble with that — with Marc, I mean — and I don't think a second public whooping would be doing us any favors.

Even though this one clearly has it coming.

"You manipulated me into bringing an innocent child into this world just to teach me a lesson?" Dahlia forces out, her voice tight.

"I had to, since nothing else was getting through to you." She leans forward and shrugs, looking unbothered. "Using Nalina was meant to be a last resort. A rather unfortunate necessity, but a necessary evil nonetheless."

Dahlia's brow scrunches. "What does Nalina have to do with any of this?"

Andrea turns to face me. "She doesn't know?"

"What don't I know?" Dahlia asks.

"Oh dear. Not only are you incapable of taking a fucking hint, but you are also just as clueless. I'll spell it out for you." Andrea leans back in her seat and crosses her slender arms over her chest. "There is only one thing Nalina Aidan loves more than money, and that's you," she says, angling her chin in Dahlia's direction. "She's hopelessly in love with you, has been for years. The poor girl is so far gone for you that she would do anything to get your attention. That includes regularly fucking my pathetic son right under your nose. How could you not have seen it?"

"Are you serious?" I ask, wriggling my fingers under Dahlia's and loosening her hold on my arm. Thankfully, she let go, and I interlace our fingers together. "For the sake of this conversation, let's just assume that she knew all along," I tell Andrea, the lie falling too quickly from my lips. "Skip to the part where you used yet another woman's feelings for your personal gain."

She heaves a patronizing breath. "In the beginning, all Nalina had to do was blackmail Curtis into telling you about the other one and this would have been over with, but that didn't work. So I asked her to put her best guy on you. I had heard nothing but great things about him and his techniques, so I fixed it so he would be at the rehearsal dinner. Then I kept paying, even after you walked out of the wedding. I was happy to pay because I didn't want you getting second thoughts and coming back, knowing my pathetic son would take you back in a heartbeat. And it worked, didn't it?

"Although I have to say that she didn't count on him falling in love with you, seeing as he had always been so anti-love and anti-commitment. Then again, as his boss and therapist, she should have known better. That was piss-poor planning on her part. Then, just when I thought I was finally free of you, you go ahead and break things off with your boy— no, *fuck* toy. And what's the first thing you did? That's right, you came running back to Curtis like some pathetic stray puppy. So you had to go again. Hence the gladiator heels, which did the trick." She lets out a self-indulgent laugh. "I should have done that from the get-go, huh?"

Dahlia's lips press into a fine line, and she swallows tightly.

As for me?

I'm done.

Really, truly done.

Neither of us should have to sit through this woman's insufferable vitriol, and I wish she would skip to the end already. Marc said it was something we wouldn't like, and I have to know how much worse it can get. If it really is worse than everything else she's already said.

"I assume there's a point to all this?" I ask.

Besides, David did say he wanted to wring the neck of the stupid fucker who put those death traps on Dahlia's feet. So I'll let him know, and he can have the pleasure of ending this bitch. I won't even feel bad about it.

"Yes, there is. It's time for my son to come home."

"Curtis finally grew some balls, huh? Good for him."

"Not Curtis. I have two sons."

With my free hand, I pinch the bridge of my nose with my thumb and forefinger. "So this is about Simone," I seethe, everything clicking into place.

Marc was right. I don't like this.

Andrea scoffs in that patronizing manner of hers. "No, this is about *Simon*. He needs to come home already." She pulls out a stack of postcards from her purse and slides them in our direction. "He's been gone long enough, don't you think? Nineteen years in self-imposed exile is enough punishment for our family. Now that the McWhorters are officially done with the Brewers, that satisfies all the terms of his absurd demands."

Neither of us says anything at first, not that there really is anything to be said. I'm the only one who moves, grabbing the cards and spreading them out on the table. Postcards, all in Simone's handwriting — dated but not postmarked, so there's no way to tell where they were sent from, just when they were sent. But the dates on the cards show these were sent over the span of eighteen years, with the most recent one dated the day of Dahlia's wedding.

"How has she been getting these to you?" I ask.

And why hasn't she sent me any? I want to ask. But I know the answer to that already. Simone didn't want me to wait for her, and in a way, I guess I did give up.

"They mostly show up at the house. Sometimes they go to Matthias's office. Curtis got them twice, but I intercepted them."

All this time Andrea has known she is alive. Yet she knowingly had Simon McWhorter declared legally dead once the statutes were up. And now she wants our help? After all this vitriol she just spewed, she really expects us to help bring her back?

And for what, exactly? More of this?

"She's not coming back," Dahlia speaks up first. There's a deathly calm to her tone, one that sends shivers running down the entire length of my spine. "The only way that will happen is over your dead bodies — yours and Matthias's. It says so in most of these postcards."

She waves us off. "It's just something he writes. I know he doesn't mean any of it, not when he's finally getting everything he wanted. Except he won't listen to me. He will only listen to you two. Only you two can make this happen."

Dahlia shakes her head. "Figure it out alone because I refuse to be party to this. Dee won't be helping you either. You wanted a dead son, and you got your wish. You don't get to change your mind about that simply because things didn't pan out the way you wanted."

"That's not true," she protests with a pained laugh. "Say what you want, but it doesn't change the fact that I love my son."

"Her name is Simone," I seethe, slamming a clenched fist on the table. "You've had nineteen years to come to terms with this. The fact that you still can't get her name or her fucking pronouns right speaks volumes about your character. So no, we want nothing to do with this."

"But—"

"But nothing," Dahlia interjects. "Did you even read these? Why would we help you when she's being very clear about this." She points to the cards before us. "All of these were addressed to you and Matthias. Nowhere does she say she will only listen to us. But it does have one resounding message spelled out. The only incentive for Simone to come back is over your dead bodies, so do everyone a favor and fucking die already."

"Hey! There's no need to be—"

She holds up a hand, silencing Andrea. "Not only are you two shitty parents but also abusive parents. If you don't want to be a mother, that's fine. That's what you hire other people for, to do all the parenting shit you don't want to do. It is not okay to take it out on them physically, emotionally, and financially. Don't forget, we were there. We saw everything. All those times you used Curtis and Simone as your personal punching bags, who do you think cleaned them up afterward? Even now, you're still using money and me to control Curtis. I'll be damned if I let you use my son as another bargaining chip in your twisted game.

"And to be clear, even if she wanted to come back, I would be the first to advise her not to. Because nothing has really changed, has it? You don't want her back because you miss her. You don't love her either. You said so yourself; you hated every moment of being a parent.

You are desperate for her return because Curtis didn't turn out to be as perfect as you had hoped. I can see the headlines — 'Prodigal Child Returns,' or some shit like that. This isn't about her; it's about you. You just want a do-over, a chance to play the perfect mother role all over again but at her expense.

"Now, just so we are all on the same page about this. The only reason Harold exists is because you wanted to fuck with me and not because you wanted to get your money's worth out of me?"

"Would you stop twisting—"

"What part of *I'm not fucking done* did you not get?" Dahlia snaps. "You had plenty of time to speak your piece; now's our chance."

Andrea's lips thin out, and they stay that way, thank fucking goodness.

"As a woman, you know what it feels like to have to endure ten months of pregnancy and its grueling effects on the body and mind, yet you thought it was okay to do the same thing to another woman? To me?

"At my rehearsal dinner, when you said to me, *'Dahlia, you really are a rare gem and I am never letting you go,'* was that also a ploy to get me away from your family or sink your hooks in deeper?

"That stunt Curtis pulled three nights before the wedding — what was that meant to teach me? And strapping four-inch gladiator heels on my swollen feet at thirty-eight weeks pregnant, what was the lesson in that?"

A minute passes, and when Andrea doesn't answer, I reach over and drum my fingers in front of her.

"Answer her, and if we don't like what you have to say, well… ask Nalina. Or better yet, ask Curtis what happens to people who piss us off."

7

———

HARRIS

I suck at being inconspicuous.

We all do.

Myself. Marc. Even David.

It's obvious why we are all here. It's because our girls are meeting with Andrea McWhorter.

That woman insisted on this sit-down, and she had been hounding Marc about it for months to make it happen. Although, as not-entertaining as this is, I get the sense that there's more to David's surly attitude than he is letting on.

"It is as we suspected," David says, his voice robotic. "They sent some people to the house. Ten, at least."

"Already taken care of," Marc says dryly, typing away at his laptop.

Hmm.

Not awkward at all.

"Did you look into the thing I asked about?" Marc adds, eyes glued to his screen.

"Of course I did. Just what do you take me for?" David's got some sass today.

"And?"

He scoffs. "Whoever she is, she's a ghost. Which, as I told you, is to be expected. If this is supposed to be some sort of test, or you are wasting my time with this—"

"Why the fuck would I waste your time with this? I wouldn't have asked if it wasn't important."

"Well, what did she do that was so unforgivable?"

"She overstepped her bounds," is all he says.

Which would be putting it mildly.

Some idiot — his name was Reuben Morelli, but I'm going with idiot instead — was running his mouth to Marc at the ball, so Marc did his thing.

By the time we got there, someone from the clean-up crew had ripped Reuben's tongue out and set it right next to his lifeless body. Then she sat next to him and waited for us, knowing there would be consequences to pay.

What irks Marc the most about it — about *her* — is that she didn't flinch when he gave her the full third degree. No one is that cool and collected, not under the great Marc Sotelo's infamous grilling. It's almost eerie, and I've never seen anything like it.

I've never met anyone like her.

Marc won't admit it, but it was a turn-on for him. *She* turned him on in a way no other woman has before, not even Delilah.

When we got back home that night, Marc fucked me. He practically dragged me into his office, locked us in there, and had his way with me. For. Hours. There was nothing gentle about it either. It was hard, ravenous, and unrelenting — like he had something to prove. Like he was staking his claim, putting his stamp on me.

Reminding himself that he had me.

Not Delilah. *Me*.

Marc and I have rough, kinky sex and/or lovemaking marathon sessions sometimes, but this was different. And it had been a long time since he did that. Since he fucked me like that.

Sixteen years, to be exact.

When he met Delilah for the first time.

This time around, *she* unknowingly unleashed the beast in him, and he needed a way to chain it back up. I couldn't deny him that, any more than I could've denied him back then. Not when I knew why he was doing it, why he needed to stake his claim on me the way that he did.

See, Marc's biggest fear is that he's too much like his father.

Lorenzo Sotelo has a type — a singular obsession, more like — and her name is Sarah Bardales. While Marc doesn't have a mom complex, he does have *his* version of a singular obsession and her name is Delilah Brewer. For the longest time, our interests aligned in that regard, until this unnamed woman disrupted that obsession with our woman, albeit briefly.

So when he shoved me against the wall of his office and kissed me hard, I let him. I let him rip the custom-made, insanely expensive suit off my body, and I didn't even protest when he used his bare hands instead of his knife. I let him force me to my knees and choke me with his cock, and I swallowed every last drop of his come as he erupted in my throat.

But that wasn't enough for him. Or me, for that matter, so I didn't protest when he bent me over his desk and fucked my lube-less ass with his fingers. I didn't protest when he practically shoved his face into my ass and ate me out until I came. Or when he dragged us both to the floor, wrapping his fingers around my throat as he fucked me raw.

Instead, I held on to him, my fingers running deep gashes in his shoulders as he rammed into me with uncharacteristic roughness, my body responding, meeting him thrust for thrust.

I love it when he loses control like that, when he gets all feral with me.

Why wouldn't I?

I love him. I love him with every fiber of my being.

When it comes down to it, Marc is to me what Simone is to Delilah. And if seventeen years with him has taught me anything, it's that I will never, ever let Marc go. I'd die for him. I'd burn for him. I'd fucking bleed for him if that's what it took to make him happy.

So what if I'm being a little too harsh with Delilah? I'd never call out someone else's name while Marc's fucking me, but that's because I always know it's him.

But it's not the same for her, so maybe I should extend her a little bit of grace. Until I get a better grasp of what's going on inside that beautiful brain of hers, something Marc figured out eons ago.

I also told Delilah all this unnamed woman — after the fact, of course — and she won't stop teasing him about it.

Although, why Marc is so intent on finding *her*, beats me.

He's even gone as far as to ask David to find her, seeing as she practically vanished after the ball.

David, for all his skills, has been hitting digital dead ends thus far, and that irks him to no end.

"Whoever this woman is, she's *the* Black Widow for the Sotelo family," he says to Marc. "It's what she does. I don't know why your dad put her on your clean-up crew or if she put herself on it. Just know that whoever trained her is the same one who trained your mother, so obviously, she's good at covering her tracks."

"So what you're saying is, you're not as good as you claim you are?" Marc tosses back.

"No, I'm saying I've tugged on a lot of strings and I keep hitting dead-ends, most of which lead to a familiar name."

Marc lets out an exasperated sigh. "Don't make me ask."

"You sure? You told me to stay the fuck away from her. Something about a felony."

I don't like the sound of this. "Nalina? Again?"

David scrunches his nose. "No, not her, although I can see where the confusion arises." He levels his gaze with Marc. "Our old *dead* friend, Dr. Sonya Goodman."

Oh yeah, that's much worse.

Besides the usual, the woman took the term Luddite to a new level. She loved paper files, so she must have hidden some things amongst her old medical files.

"I don't see what the problem is," I say in an attempt to put a positive spin on this. "We have the files. All you need is—"

"No," David bites. "I'm not using Dahlia like that again. I would rather ask Delilah, but you've made it clear you don't want either of them to know about this. So find another way."

Marc sighs. "What else did you find?"

"Nothing. She's a ghost. There was one strange thing, though. She's listed as the backup billing contact for a Cryobank account, with Dr. Goodman being the main one. That account is still current, as far as I can tell, even though Dr. Goodman has been dead for years. It's also the only account tied to her name, so either someone else is paying all of her other bills, or she's gone to a lot of trouble to fly under the radar and has a vested interest in keeping things that way. Are you absolutely sure you want me to keep going down this path?"

"I never took you for a wuss," I tell him. If someone has to challenge him, to keep him on his toes, it might as well be me.

"I'm barely staying above-board with everything else, but if I keep tugging these threads it will take me down the path of the things you don't want to know about. I made a promise to my girl, okay? This goes against that promise, so I need to know it will be worth it. Because let's face it. We were all thinking about ripping Reuben's tongue out of its socket, and you're just mad that she beat you to it."

Marc scowls. "It'll be worth it."

David studies him for a beat. "Your dad and Dr. Goodman were chummy for decades. This means I'll have to dig around your family's business. No holds barred, no exceptions, and that includes your law firm's files. And I have to tell Dahlia about this because a promise is a promise, and I'm a man of my word. Will you have a problem with that?"

He mumbles noncommittally.

"Great."

Then we go right back to silence.

The fuckers.

"This is stupid," I tell them after some time passes. "The girls are doing okay, no claws in sight. This whole exchange is being recorded, and we have men stationed throughout the restaurant. Everything is under control. Since we are all here, why don't we hash out what the fuck it is that's bothering you two. Starting with you, David."

He looks away and bites the inside of his cheek.

"No? Okay then. Marc, why don't you bring David up to speed on your conversation with Hurricane Dahlia."

"What the fuck, H?" Marc hisses.

I wave a hand in David's direction. "He knows."

"And I told Dahlia that they needed to handle their shit between the two of them," Marc adds.

"What the fuck did you say to her?" David bites.

Here we go.

"Why do you assume I said anything to her?"

"Because you always do. Last weekend was a fluke, wasn't it? The whole truce thing is a fucking joke. It's been barely seven days, and you're back to your old tricks."

"David—"

"Where would she get the idea that she's not enough for me? If you didn't put that shit in her head—"

"I'm going to stop you right there," I interject. "She went to him, okay? Not the other way around. That's a ballsy move, so I can't even be mad about it. She could have come to me, but no. She went to the

King of Shooting People Down and she shot her shot. I can't help but respect that, you know?"

"Dahlia wouldn't—"

"If you don't believe it, check her fucking phone. I know you still have that recording program installed."

He huffs out a breath. "That's beside the point. She would've told me if she wasn't satisfied—"

"Dude, she wouldn't. And neither would you. It wasn't about her; it was about you. Although I find it interesting that she didn't go to Delilah first, she went straight to Marc. He could've turned her down. He didn't have to entertain that conversation. But he took the time to explain it to her, and she still wants to do it. For you. Hence, the reason why she's sitting over there with that insufferable woman."

We all turn to look at said insufferable woman with identical scowls on our faces. With the way Dahlia's fingers are digging into Delilah's arm, I can only imagine Andrea is saying something stupid again. I only hope Dahlia finally puts the great Andrea McWhorter in her fucking place.

That's a show I'd pay good money to see.

"Also, Dahlia was right about everything," I quietly add.

"Urgh. Don't start with the love thing," David objects hotly.

"But all I want to talk about is the *love* thing, asshole. We don't keep you around because of your money or your looks, although your face is pretty to look at."

"Right," he drawls. "I'm sure that's all it is."

"We've avoided the subject for years. Even now, we're still dancing around the topic."

"What do you want me to say?"

"You don't have to say anything. But recognize that your girl loves you and is willing to do whatever it takes to make you happy. Including that." I wave a hand in their direction. "Even including this. All Marc did was explain to her what it would entail. Because I sure as fuck wouldn't have done that, and neither would you. So knock it off with the passive-aggressive shit and talk things over with her, or else—"

The crack of skin against skin fills the room. We all turn to see Dahlia on her feet, chest heaving, arm in the air. Delilah's fingers curl around her arm while Andrea cups her left cheek with both palms, a fearful expression filtering through her face.

Marc mutters, "Not again," under his breath.
David's hearty laugh fills in the space. "That's my girl."
"At least we're not in a police station this time," I add.
We've all done worse things, especially Marc.
I see his point, though. This will be a headache to deal with.

8

—————

MARC

"I really hope this means we're square," Captain Evelyn says as she gestures to one of her officers. The guy in question nods before excusing himself, closing the door behind him with a gentle click.

My guess would be he's headed for the holding cells.

Taking a long swig of the bad police station coffee, I try to muster up some semblance of empathy for her situation, but there is none to be had. "Not by a long shot. But it's a start."

"A start? This is the second documented incident in eight months. Your clients can't just go around publicly assaulting people and expect there to be no repercussions."

She's one to talk.

Her idiot brother's shenanigans keep putting her in my debt, all because she takes this *blood-is-thicker-than-water* mantra way too seriously.

I mean, I do too. I just happen to be a lot more selective about the people I'd lay down my life for. Or compromise on my principles.

"Let's not get ahead of ourselves now, shall we? And while you're at it, check your math. We were more than square the first time," I say, referring to the first incident, the one where Delilah beat Nalina to a bloody pulp right at this station.

It happened in one of the visitors' waiting rooms they were so graciously granted. There were no cameras in the room, thank goodness, but the commotion they were making was loud enough to draw the attention of two off-duty officers. They pulled Delilah off of a bloodied Nalina, and Nalina gave one of them a black eye for her trouble.

Charging the *victim* with assaulting a police officer would've looked bad for everyone involved — not to mention, Nalina probably is romantically involved with the officer she punched — so Evelyn swept the whole incident under the rug.

For all her bitching and whining, compared to that, this incident is a walk in the park.

The only reason why we're here is because Andrea McWhorter is the *victim* this time around.

Victim.

The thought is laughable.

If only they knew their so-called victims were the villains in the Brewer twins's story.

"…our business is done after this," Evelyn is saying.

It's the same thing she says every time. Except she's forgetting one thing — a crooked cop is a crooked cop; in Captain Evelyn's case, there is much to be leveraged.

"Is that what you think?" Her lips part and I hold up a hand to stop her. "Don't bother; that was a rhetorical question. Putting Dahlia in a holding cell was a bit much. We both know there won't be a paper trail for this."

"My point exactly." The undertones of sarcasm in her voice don't escape me. "This means we're square, Marc Sotelo."

"We were, then your precious brother reset the clock on your debt, and then some." I set the mug down on her messy desk. "It's not my fault he keeps digging himself deeper into a hole he has no hope of crawling out of. Or that you keep throwing yourself in the line of fire for a lost cause."

"Would you turn your back on family?"

"Of course not. That's how we arrived at this tedious stalemate. The difference is I can keep my family in check. You? Not so much. Your brother is out of control. At some point, you're going to have to accept you can't save him from himself."

"But you can," she counters.

"For now, yes. Not forever." I stand and head for the door. "I put him in a treatment facility in Moorhead. His mandatory thirty-day stay ends in a week, but it would be in his best interest to extend it another thirty days. And don't worry about the cost, it's all paid for. What he does after that is up to him. We can't force him to stay clean if he doesn't want that for himself. Nor can we keep him from dealing. Know that the moment he puts himself in my father's crosshairs, I can't help him anymore."

I shouldn't be dispensing advice, but I can't be too picky.

Besides, she's right. Like her, there's nothing I wouldn't do for my family. And I have done some pretty terrible things, too. I'd do it all over again with no regrets.

As I step outside the station, the panic in Harris's voice gives me pause.

"Why are you doing this?" he asks Delilah.

They're standing in the middle of the parking lot, and he has both of Delilah's hands in his. But not in an *I want to hurt you* type of way. It's more like an *"I'm going to keep you from running away"* type of deal, which is absurd because Delilah isn't going anywhere.

Until she counters with an, "We could use some space from each other."

"What? No. That's the last thing I want."

"What *you* want? God, you're so fucking selfish." She scoffs as she pulls her hands from his, but he tightens his hold on her. "Let go."

He shakes his head. "Not until you take it back."

"No. It's not about what you want, Harris. It's about what *I* need. And right now, we could use some fucking space."

Dahlia and David stand off to the side, both leaning against her car and pretending not to be observing this exchange.

I'd be lying if I said this whole thing wasn't giving me an eerie sense of déjà vu.

The Brewer twins and Harris really will be the death of me.

"Please, don't do this," Harris pleads. "I'm sorry for what I said."

"No, you're not." The chilly spring breeze blows a strand of her brown hair over her eyes, and she huffs out a breath. "If you were, we wouldn't be having this conversation here."

"Fine. I'm not sorry. That doesn't mean you should leave."

Leave?

I've heard enough.

"H?" I call out.

He tenses up at my voice, and Delilah uses that opening to yank both hands out of his, then ducks out of his reach as she makes a beeline for me. She pauses to peer deep into my eyes before snaking her arms around my waist.

I feel my own heart thundering against my ribcage as her body melts into mine; and as she lays her cheek over my heart. I feel her chest swelling as she breathes me in. It feels like a goodbye, and I don't want it to be. So I bury my face in the nook of her nape and draw in a deep breath, her sweet peppermint scent flooding my senses.

"What was that about?" I whisper into the shell of her ear.

She leans back, then trails the back of her finger along the edge of my chin. "I'm going home with Daa."

I got that part, and I could do what Harris did just moments prior. Or I could do something else.

Instead, I say, "Okay."

Her hand falls off my face, and she frowns slightly. "That's it? You're not going to talk me out of it like Harris did?"

I shake my head, keeping my features schooled as I cup her cheeks. "As tempting as it sounds, I can't keep you chained to us against your will," I admit, even though it kills me to say the words out loud. "You need space, so take it. Take as long as you need. We'll be here. We're not going anywhere."

A beat passes, and then she goes up on her tiptoes and kisses me softly before backing off. I force myself to watch as she climbs into the back seat of Dahlia's car, taking note of how she purposefully avoids Harris's gaze. I also force myself to watch as they drive off, even though everything inside me screams that I put a stop to this.

Then I grit my teeth as I turn to Harris, my already frayed patience wearing thin. "What the fuck did you say to her?"

9

DELILAH

"You know I'll do anything for you, sweetheart," David tells my sister, "but you're asking me to do the impossible, and I can't do that. We're happy, Dahlia. Why muddy up the waters?"

I shouldn't be eavesdropping on what is a private conversation.

Lord knows I shouldn't, but I can't seem to help myself.

They're sort of talking about me, and I'd be lying if I said I wasn't getting a strong sense of déjà vu.

The difference is that they're not discussing kicking me out, and it's a relief. David isn't as big of an asshole as Marc is. Don't get me wrong, he does have his asshole-ish moments from time to time, but there's no denying that he loves my sister. He worships the ground she walks on. He's obsessed with her and everything that makes her happy.

And, as it so happens, I make her happy.

I'm her identical twin sister, her womb mate. We're linked, as it should be, in ways that defy the laws of logic. And I'm not above playing that up to my full advantage every chance I get.

Sometimes, I use it to get away from my men, even if it's only for a brief reprieve from them.

"Marc was very thorough in explaining how this works," Dahlia says. "He told me to tread lightly with this, that this is just what Nalina would use to get between us."

"He's not wrong," David acquiesces. "I don't want her anywhere near you."

"And I don't want her anywhere near you either."

"That won't be an issue. I will never, ever go back to her."

I believe him, but I can tell Dahlia has her doubts.

Given her history with Curtis, I'm not surprised. That asshole did a number on her. He cheated on her repeatedly with some of our friends and most of our colleagues — people we have to work with.

"I'm not going anywhere," David assures her. "I don't see anyone else but you. You're it for me, Dahlia. I'm head over heels in love with you. I love our son and plan to spend the rest of my life with you both. What do I need to do to prove all that to you?"

"Nothing, David. You don't have to prove your love for me; you already do every day. I love you, more than you could ever know, but I also know what it's like to live a lie." There's a pause, her words carrying a weighted undertone. "I know what it's like to shut down such a big part of yourself to protect the ones you love. That's not something I want for you, and I refuse to force you to live that lie with me."

His groan of frustration reaches me. "Is this about what Andrea said?"

"That's part of it, yes. Everyone but me knows that Nalina has a thing for me. I thought she was using me to get to you. It never occurred to me that it was the other way around. There's also the matter where I don't feel bad for her, even knowing that Andrea used those feelings to control her. What does that make me then?"

"Human, sweetheart. It makes you human. Not only is Dr. Aidan a predator, but she also made money off of it. Lots and lots of it, and you know that I didn't take monetary compensation. If it helps, I don't feel bad for her either. She had it coming. Sure, it bruised her ego, but she'll get over it."

"I'm sure she will. Here's the thing, though. I didn't know she liked me because I didn't want to know. For as long as I've known her, she'd look for excuses to touch me, and after a while, I stopped being subtle about cringing from her touch. I kept blinders on, David, on purpose. I intentionally ignored that part of my sexuality on purpose. It wouldn't be fair of me to expect the same of you."

"You know, Marc's been saying cryptic shit for months; things like you and I are more alike than I thought. I already knew, through. I know you're attracted to women—"

"Not women, David. *Woman*. Just one, and she's taken." A beat passes, then, "You must think I'm pathetic, huh?"

Pathetic?

If anyone's pathetic in this scenario, that would be me.

How did I not see it?

My feet move of their own accord, propelling me to their bedroom.

"Why didn't you say anything?" I blurt out.

They both turn to face me. Dahlia, from her position on the bed with a haakaa silicone breast pump hanging off her right breast. David was pacing the room with baby Harold fast asleep in his arms.

"I'm sorry. I should've knocked." The words tumble out of me in a rush as I step into the room. "Hell, I know I probably should've done many things differently, but... umm... why didn't you say anything?"

Her golden brown eyes are sullen as she watches me. "It wouldn't have made a difference."

Maybe, maybe not. Still, it would've been nice to know.

All this time, I've been so focused on my grief, on my pain, that I never considered how Dahlia was affected by her absence. I felt it, thanks to our bond, but I didn't dwell on it. At first, it was drowned in my pain, then numbed with my medication.

It's been years, though. I have no excuse now.

"You don't know that," I eventually say.

A wave of regret washes over her face. "We were children, Dee. I was with Curtis. It wouldn't have made a difference."

All valid points, I want to say, but something else comes out instead. "We don't keep secrets from each other. You should've told me."

David's gaze darts back and forth between us. "I'll put Harold in his room."

He brushes past me, and all I can do is watch him walk away, leaving the door open behind him.

That was a smart move on his part.

The cat is out of the bag on this one. Like it or not, it's not a bell that can be unrung.

"It was safer not to say anything," Dahlia says once he's gone. "I could never hurt you like that. I may as well drive a stake through my heart. Besides, as I said, it wouldn't have made a difference. Simone's in love with you, not me."

Looking back, I'm not so sure it was one-sided. The signs were always there, but like her, I kept blinders on.

I wonder briefly if this makes me a monster. Simone didn't just leave me; she left all of us. She didn't just turn her back on me; she turned her back on everything and everyone she's ever known.

Her reasons, whatever they may be, were valid — *are* valid, but I don't care anymore. She needs to come home already, it's been nineteen fucking years. And if that makes me a monster, so be it. I'm a monster. I can live with that.

I make my way to their bed and sit next to her. "Marc will bring her back if I ask him to. I'm sure of it."

Dahlia sighs as she pulls the haakaa off her right breast and attaches it to the other. "Is that what you want?"

Maybe. Maybe not. But what choice do I have?

The wedge between Harris and myself grows deeper with each passing day. Sooner or later, Marc will be fed up with me, too, and he'll take it back.

"This would be a good thing, right? For both of you?" David points out as he walks into the room, closing the door behind him.

"Not necessarily," Dahlia adds, her palm encircling the freed breast as she jiggles it enticingly for him.

His vibrant amber eyes sparkle in the evening light, heavy-lidded with his lust as he makes his way over to us. Then he remembers I'm in the room and pauses mid-step.

It's hard work bitting back the smile that forms. "Don't stop on my account."

She shrugs and scoots back on the bed, leaning against the headboard. He climbs in after and settles in next to her. She watches as he gently disengages the haakaa off her left breast and sets it down on the side table. He covers both of her breasts with his hands and simultaneously massages them. She presses the back of her head against the headboard, her eyelids fluttering close as a soft moan slips past her lips.

"It feels strange," she whispers, then clears her throat. "We've never done this with an audience."

"And you proposed a threesome with us? Or is it a five-some? David, how does the math work?"

"Same way it always does," he answers, keeping a steady rhythm with his hands. "Boy meets girl—"

"Honey, you know that's not what she's asking," Dahlia interjects, her eyes meeting mine. "I know we need this, but David has his reservations."

"I heard. You know the guys would kill to get their hands on you again," I tell him. "I know it's been years, but Harris still talks about that thing you do with your tongue."

Dahlia glares at me. "I hate you."

"No, you don't," I say with a laugh, staring at her breasts. "You love me. The guys love David. And I love watching. There's so much to be learned by just watching."

"I have an idea. You've never had two people touching you at the same time, and since you are comfortable with both of us—"

"Dude! You're not *actually* suggesting that I have sex with my sister, are you?"

He turns to me, the horrified expression on his face almost comical. "That's where your mind went? Jesus, Delilah."

I lift a curious brow. "Are you saying you don't have a twin fetish?"

"Most guys do, but that's not what I was going to propose." He pats the space next to her. "Just come over here, would you? We will both touch her at the same time. Strictly clinical touches, if that puts your mind at ease. As long as Dahlia is okay with it, of course."

Dahlia worries her bottom lip but nods.

He turns to me. "What do you say?"

They're both watching me with identical expectant gazes.

"I'll do you one better," I say instead, crawling over to them. "Ever since you brought it up at Christmas, I've been curious about what breastmilk tastes like. It'll be a strictly clinical feeding, of course. As long as you're okay with it."

10

DELILAH

That first taste hits me hard.

Dahlia tenses in my arms, and I'm half-expecting her to push me away in disgust. Her reluctance is short-lived, though, and she wraps her arms around me, fingers spearing through my scalp as she fuses my face to her breast.

"More," she breathes.

Something shifts in me at her command, and I latch on harder.

This is strictly clinical, I remind myself.

But she tastes so fucking sweet, and she grips me tighter as her milk flows down my throat.

Someday, our roles will be reversed.

Will Marc and Harris want to drink from me? Will David?

Will Dahlia?

I think she would. I know I do.

Purely clinical, my mind scolds as Dahlia's moans pierced through the haze, spurring me on. It's too easy to get lost in the pleasurable sensations, in someone else's satisfaction and happiness.

For someone like me, happiness is overrated. And I'm just settling into a comfortable routine when something else happens. In my mind's eye, I stop seeing my twin, and, as always, someone else takes her place.

My soulmate takes her place.

This time, it feels real — too real to be a mirage.

It doesn't feel like a shroud, either. It feels like a memory, one I want to live in forever.

There's a special place in hell for people like me. Because as I'm clinging to my sister's breast, I'm imagining she's my not-dead fiancée instead.

"I wish I could have breasts like yours," Simone's smooth voice washes over me, wrapping my defective body up in a warm cocoon as she thrusts upward into me.

In the present, I squeeze my thighs together as I feel the dampness building between my legs.

It's too real.

A throwback, perhaps?

"You will, someday," I answer in earnest, my fingernails raking into the soft flesh of her pale stomach. "Then I'll get to suck on them anytime I want and as much as I want."

Though clouded with lust, her violet eyes search mine in earnest. "You can start now."

Her voice, a mere whisper, stuns me.

"Are you sure?" I groan, rolling my hips to get her as deep as possible.

My gaze drops to the pink pebbled tips, a stark contrast to her pale white skin. My mouth waters at the sight. She's been on estrogen for some time now, and it shows. I'm on top of her because her nipples are delectable but also incredibly sensitive, sometimes to the point where they hurt.

When she hurts, I hurt. And nothing about this is supposed to hurt.

A warm hand envelopes my cheek, forcing my eyes back to hers. "Yes, I am. I wouldn't have said it if I wasn't sure."

I don't need to be told a third time. She knows I've been dying to do this for some time now, long before she started hormone therapy years ago. She's also self-conscious about her body, so everything we do sexually is at her pace.

Leaning forward, I close my mouth over her left nipple, swirling my tongue around the tip before latching on and sucking hard. She moans and arches into the sensation; an involuntary shudder racks her body.

"That feels fucking amazing," she murmurs softly. "We should've done this sooner."

My lips stretch into a smile, and my bottom teeth graze the hardened nub.

"Easy, tiger," she breathes. "I'll bite back."

"Ouch," Dahlia's voice pierces through the haze, her voice scratching at my skin. "Dee, slow down."

"Huh?" I whimper around her nipple, my eyes finally reaching up to look at her.

My mirage disappears, and my sister takes her place.

No, no, no, no, no, no, no.

Dahlia's lips move against the air, but I don't catch what she's saying. My subconscious refuses to release its claws from my reality, pulling me deeper and deeper into a past I so desperately want to reside in for just a little longer.

I want to stay with Simone a little longer, yet every breath I take fills my lungs with the haunting scent that lingers — a cruel reminder of a love that flourishes in this space.

My chest heaves as I struggle to pull oxygen into my lungs. If my mind were less chaotic and more settled, I would use any of the breathing exercises Mom and Dad taught me a lifetime ago. I'm not sure if it'd make a difference, though, as my panic attacks stopped eons ago, and Dahlia got them in my stead.

"Something's wrong," Dahlia's mumbled whisper filters through the memory I'm drowning in, tugging me back to the present inch by struggling inch.

Warm hands spread over the middle of my back — an unfamiliar touch that soothes the ache in my bones.

David's, I believe.

His finger tickles the corner of my mouth, slowly inching past my lips. "Ease up a little."

I release her nipple with a pop. "What?"

"You bit her hard enough to draw blood," David says. "The only one who gets bitten around here is me."

I shrug and lean back in to take her nipple in my mouth, but she cups my cheeks with both palms and pulls me back. "You're shaking, Dee. Where's your head at?"

Here, with you. In the past, with her.

The words stay stuck on my tongue, and so does something else.

"There's blood on your tongue," Dahlia says, her thumbs running soothingly against my cheek. "My blood. Do you not taste that?"

My breathing slows, and so does the rush of blood to my ears. I give her a slight shake of my head as I take in her gorgeous face, using it as an anchor until the gasping subsides. Her jaw is clenched tight, eyes filled with concern as she studies me. I can tell the moment realization dawns.

"You were thinking about Simone," she states, her voice thick with emotion.

Looking at her is the literal equivalent of staring in a mirror. I was never good at lying to my other half, and I'm not about to start now.

"She consumes me," I admit, my voice trembling slightly. "I thought I had it under control, but... I... can't shake this feeling, this never-ending descent into chaos."

"How long has this been going on?"

My brow furrows. "I'm not sure. It's like my mind is playing a cruel game, fracturing every thought into tiny shards that are impossible to piece back together. I see her everywhere I go, like a mirage constantly slipping out of my reach. I feel her touch everywhere, but it's fleeting, like trying to hold onto water. That feeling slips away, leaving me drowning in this abyss of confusion. It's getting worse, and I'm afraid if I don't do anything about it, I'll become too broken to be fixed."

"You're not broken, Dee."

"It certainly feels like it. It's tearing me apart from within. I'm fucking scared. I'm terrified that this chaos will never cease, that I'll be forever lost within this labyrinth of my mind."

She laces her fingers behind my neck and pulls our foreheads together. "I won't let you. You're not alone in this. I'm right here with you. I am a part of you, and you are a part of me. We're linked. We share this burden. Where you go, I go. No matter how dark the night is, I will always come for you, and I'm pretty sure that's coded into the fine print of our shared DNA."

The bed dips next to us, the heat of David's body filling our shared space. He puts an arm around Dahlia, his other hand squeezes my thigh, and his thumb draws comforting circles.

The silence hangs heavy between us, thick with unspoken words.

"She needs to come home," Dahlia declares, breaking the tension that wraps around us like a suffocating cloak.

That's the understatement of the century.

"Marc already asked me to look into it," David adds.

"When?"

He shrugs. "A week after the Sotelo ball. It's been moving at a snail's pace since we've been otherwise occupied."

I let out a strained laugh. "What about you, Daa? Will you be okay?"

Dahlia leans back, and her eyes meet mine, filled with sorrow and understanding. "She's yours, okay? I'm not your competition."

Something tells me it won't be that simple.

Then again, nothing about Simone was ever simple.

11

———

MARC

"Anything?" Harris asks for the umpteenth time.

He's been hovering at the foot of the stairs, constantly interrupting me as I'm trying to get some work done.

"Not since the last time you asked," I glance at the clock icon on my laptop, "ten fucking minutes ago."

"So? You know where she is. Go get her. Bring her back home, where she belongs."

I suppose there's something to be said about getting older and wiser. A year ago, I would've done just that and not given a second thought as to how my actions affected the people around me.

It's irrational.

I know it is.

Still, I can't help it. After all, it's been seventy-two fucking hours, and she's still at Dahlia's and David's place. Which, technically, is her place too — or rather, hers and Dahlia's, since their parents left it for them.

To make matters tense, there hasn't been a peep from her — hence Harris's hovering.

Whatever happened between them a few days ago, it's had him mopping around the house. Except he refuses to accept responsibility for his part in it, choosing to focus instead on the hurt. All because she called him by Simone's name again, and that hurt his fragile feelings.

Oh, how badly I wanted to shake him. To tell him to grow the fuck up.

This time around, I shrugged and countered with, "We've already established that your selfishness knows no bounds, and I refuse to alienate our future wife because of it. She'll come home on her own accord, so I suggest you make yourself scare until I talk to her."

He huffs out his frustration and leaves for his basement workshop. With any luck, he'll stay down there for the next seventy-two hours. Not long enough to cool his fucking jets, but enough to teach him a lesson in *think before you speak*.

That, and Delilah is ours.

Nothing and no one is ever going to change that.

She's not going anywhere. This family of ours, we're going to add to it. We're going to expand it, not shrink it.

Harris can have his doubts, reservations, whatever. That's his prerogative.

I don't.

As far as I'm concerned, Delilah has been mine for the last sixteen years. All of her. Body, heart, and soul. I don't fuck around when I want something. From the day I met her, I wanted to claim her. I wanted to fuck her, to possess her, to mark her perfect body with my knife, my mouth, my cock, and, more importantly, my cum. I wanted to hear her scream my name as she fell apart above, underneath, and with me.

It took a fucking eternity for us to get there, but I have done all of those things to her.

And she does.

It's my name she screams every time I fuck her, not Simone's.

I should've asked him what, exactly, it was that he was doing wrong, but I held my tongue. Truth is, I warned him months ago. Either he takes what Delilah is offering, or he leaves her the fuck alone. It's not that hard to comprehend. She was clear on where we stood in her life and in her heart. She was candid that she wasn't some prize to be won, yet he turned it into a competition anyway.

If she's calling him by her name, he has no one to blame for that but himself.

Granted, I didn't tell him about her pregnancy. Knowing him, he'll find a way to turn that into yet another contest.

My phone chimes, and it's David.

David: I told her everything in the interest of full disclosure.

Marc: Did you two discuss the other thing?

Three dots appear, disappear, then appear again.

David: Depends.

Then the fucker leaves it at that.
A minute later, I sent a single sentence.

Marc: What the fuck does 'depends' mean?

David: Delilah was curious, so we fooled around a little. Something happened—

I stopped reading and hit the call button.

"You did *what*?" I practically scream.

"You're on speaker, asshole. Behave," David's voice filters through, too casual for my liking.

"And you crossed a line, jackass. Whatever happened to fucking boundaries?"

"Why would you write that, knowing it'd only piss him off?" Dahlia's amused tone answers, addressing him. "It's not what you think, Marc," she continues, addressing me. "Dee had an episode, is all. I suspect this wasn't the first time."

"We talked about this, and David fucking knows better. Why was he fooling around with her in the first place?"

"It wasn't him, Marc. It was me."

Oh.

My anger deflates. "How? What happened?"

"David feeds from me, and she was only going to watch at first, but she got curious. This is why you need to be clearer about these things, honey," she's telling David. "No boundaries were crossed. And Marc, don't go reading into it. It wasn't a twin-on-twin sex thing. It was a strictly clinical feeding."

I'd be lying if I said my mind didn't conjure up *that* image. "How did that lead to an episode?"

"Well, she zoned out and bit me hard enough to draw blood. David got her off my nipple, but she was pretty out of it for a little bit. She kept mumbling Simone's name too. How long has this been going on, and why didn't you tell me?"

"She's been under a lot of stress. This business with Andrea certainly wasn't helping things."

"Well, thank goodness that's done now," she breathes, and I don't have the heart to tell her it's far from over. "Dee has been taking her medication regularly, right?"

"She's never skipped a dose. She's low, though."

"I know. Her six-month refill arrived at the house a week ago, so she's set. You didn't answer my question, Marc. How long has this been going on?"

I blow out a breath and close my laptop. "The episodes started after she watched Simone's tapes."

There's a pause on the other line. "Can you do it? Can you bring Simone back?" Her voice, a mere whisper, filters through the phone. Fragile, yet carrying a torrent of emotions.

I set my laptop aside. "She has to say the words."

"'I want her back'. That's all you need, correct?"

I can't help the chuckle that bubbles up. "D needs to say the words, not you."

"She's my identical twin. We're practically the same person. I'm saying the words. Shouldn't that be enough?"

"On principle, no. Before you say any more, know that H made a case for it, and I told him the same thing."

"Is that why you asked David to start looking months ago?"

Urgh.

David and his fucking big mouth. "He wasn't supposed to tell you that."

"Well, he did, so tough shit. Like you, we don't keep secrets from each other."

Dahlia sure learns fast.

"Bringing Simone back will also affect the dynamics of your and David's relationship. Does he know that you're in love with her too?"

A beat passes, then, "He knows," she admits, her voice barely audible.

"We know what's at stake, and we trust each other," David says. "As for the other thing, we're on the same page. We want to move forward—"

"What he means to say is we don't want Nalina anywhere near David or me," Dahlia interjects with a laugh. "Do whatever you need to do to make this happen. Before you try to talk me out of it, David already said it won't be easy. I'm willing to learn, and I'm a quick study. Oh, and Dee should be home soon. Your driver picked her up an hour ago."

As if on cue, I hear footsteps.

Hers.

I'd recognize the pep in her step anywhere.

"Speak of the angel," I say as Delilah comes into view. "She just walked in."

"Don't let her beat herself up about what happened. She did plenty of that already," Dahlia finishes by way of goodbye.

"Take care," I say with a smile before hanging up.

Delilah leans against the doorway, watching me. "Was that Daa and David? Were they checking up on me?"

"It wasn't like that. Come here," I beckon.

She drops her purse on the coffee table and makes her way over to the switch, flipping them and plunging us both into darkness. Then she makes her way over to me. Reaching for her arm, I pull her onto my lap and nuzzle my face into the crook of her neck.

"Are we multitasking again?"

Despite myself, I smile. "Not today, no. I just missed you, is all."

"Uh-huh. Harris put you up to this, didn't he?"

"Not really," I whisper against her skin. "Happy one-year anniversary."

Her breath hitches. "You remembered."

"I remember every second of us," I tell her because it's the truth. "Don't tell me you—"

"No," she says, a little too forcefully. "It's impossible for me to forget anything. My brain just isn't wired that way. Not even with meds."

It's the fourth time in two weeks that she's not-so-casually referenced her medication in conversation. "Is it time to adjust them?"

Her head rolls against my shoulder. "It's a lifetime prescription. Changing them would be a logistical nightmare, with the added complication that the prescribing doctor is deceased."

The hairs on my back stand still. "Sonya?"

She nods but doesn't say anything else.

"We know what's in them, and we can get someone else to—"

"Not for this exact combination. No formulary has the permission or expertise to change it."

"So not FDA-approved then."

"Not necessarily. My parents were researchers, and they put this particular combo together. Sonya found a dispensary to issue them. She also monitored how I was doing while on them, and there was never a need to adjust them. I know what's in them, and I don't care. They help me function, Marc. They keep me together. Without them, I would've fallen apart nineteen years ago, and that would've cost three people their lives. Including mine. Then we wouldn't be here today, doing this." She bounces on my lap, her intent clear.

"D…" I groan, my half-mast cock instantly hardening.

I can feel her lips stretch into a smile. "I don't want to talk about my meds," she says softly, and her fingers move to my belt. "I can think of a million other ways to spend our first anniversary."

I place my hands over hers. Under different circumstances, I wouldn't turn her down, but she's hiding something, and I want to know what. The quickest way to extract that information is not to give her what she wants.

"I thought you missed me," she pouts.

"I did."

"So what's the issue? I need you to fuck me, Marc. Make it hurt."

I reach across the chair and flip the soft lamp on the side.

She blows out a breath on my neck. "What are you doing?"

"I want to see your face."

"Why?"

"You are so fucking beautiful, D. I missed you. I missed looking at you."

I did miss her, but not for pure intentions.

There's a special place in hell for people like me. More specifically, men like me.

Men who let things get too far with women they shouldn't touch in the first place. Then again, where she's concerned, there has always been a relentless ache that resides deep within me, a magnetic pull that defies all reason and convention.

She leans back, her eyes squeezed shut. I can see the metaphorical wheels turning in her head. I slide a warm hand up the side of her face, and I can immediately tell she's resisting the urge to lean into it.

"Look at me, D."

She doesn't. A beat passes, then I repeat. "Darling, look at me."

Her eyelids part, and then her throat shifts.

What I see in them knocks the air out of my lungs.

Her eyes, pools of vulnerability, meet mine in a silent plea for understanding. The intensity in her eyes mirrors the turmoil within me — the conflict between what she's asking of me and the knowledge that I'll enjoy every moment of doling out the punishment she so vehemently desires.

Anytime she uses the phrase *Make it hurt*, it's almost always followed by some variation of *Because I deserve it*. But not because she thinks herself as defective for loving Simone, that much I deduced months ago. It's almost always something else.

"If it's punishment you want, I'll be more than happy to give you that," I grunt, my thrusts shallowing. "But I need to know exactly what you want to be punished for."

She worries her bottom lip. "I slept with David and Dahlia," she murmurs softly.

"That sounds like an oversimplification of events." I press down on her chin and release the tender flesh between her teeth. "David and Dahlia told me what happened."

A sigh of resignation slips past her lips. "I know we haven't agreed on anything official yet, and technically it's cheating, but—"

"It wasn't," I grit as I thread my fingers through her scalp and grab fistfuls of her hair. "I hoped you would talk with your sister. As much as H and I want David, the whole thing is moot if Dahlia isn't on board or comfortable with all of us."

She pauses, her golden brown eyes frosting. "So you want to fuck her? Is that it? We're identical, so it shouldn't be that fucking hard."

The weight of her words settles over me like a suffocating cloak. My movements go still. "I'm not in the habit of forcing myself on women, D," I say, my voice thick with emotion. "I am not my father."

Her eyes soften. "I'm sorry," she whispers, her voice trembling slightly. "I shouldn't have said that. I'm just…"

"Protective of your twin, I know," I finish for her. "Trust me, I get it. She's never been in an open relationship, and neither have you."

"What would you call what we are?" She asks, wrapping her fingers around my wrists.

"We're a closed throuple." I loosen my hold on her, keeping my fingers in her hair. "Just because H and I have a history with David doesn't mean this will be easy for you both."

"We're geniuses. How hard can it be?"

"Hard. It's a steep learning curve, and we will all fuck shit up several times."

"Great. When do we start?"

"After we all meet to go over the rules. But first, we need to talk about what happened three nights ago. David said you were in some trance last night when you fed from Dahlia."

She pulls my hands out of her hair and climbs off my lap. "It's not what you think."

I lean forward and reach for her, but she ducks out of my grasp. "I believe you, D, but I need to know where your mind went."

"Same place it always goes," she answers, and I can tell it's the truth. She walks over to where she set down her purse earlier, picks it up, and loops it over her shoulder. "On a scale of zero to go pound rocks, how pissed off is Harris?"

"I don't know about pissed off, but I asked him to make himself scarce until we talked."

Her shoulders slump. "That's probably wise." She half-turns to face me. "Do I wait for you in our playroom or go straight to bed?"

I stand and, in a few strides, close the distance between us. "Option 1, if that's what you really want."

A tentative smile graces her lips as she reaches out, her hand finding mine with a comforting grasp. "It is. I promise."

12

MARC

"You got what you wanted, Andrea," I say, my fingers tightening around my phone as I hold it to my ear. "That means our business is done."

"That was Phase one," is her gleeful response. "A crack in the façade, as you lawyers would say."

"Your overpriced, incompetent lawyer has been giving you bad advice. It wasn't a crack or a façade. It was the door slamming shut."

"So you say," she quips. "Like it or not, I plan on being a thorn in your side until I get what I'm owed."

I can feel the vein in my temple pulsing with the red-hot blaze of my anger. "For the last time, you cannot take legal action against the twins for a deal their parents made with your in-laws."

"That's Matthias's intention, not mine."

"Then tell your husband he has no case. Or better yet, tell your lawyer that. Or waste your money and our time with this. Just know that any judge worth their salt would laugh you out of their courtroom."

"Oh, I'm not concerned about that. I prefer another sit-down with the twins, as I originally requested. Now that we got the first one out of the way, facilitating the next one should be easy. Say, in three months?"

Three months?

I hold the phone before me, fantasizing about tossing it to the wall. The satisfaction to be gained from the act would be short-lived, and I'll be left with the headache of replacing the damn thing and getting it re-encrypted. Plus, listening to David's smartass comments on top of that isn't worth the hassle.

How I wish I didn't have to deal with this woman.

"I'll take your silence to mean your acquiescence," Andrea's voice filters through the silence. "We'll see you in three months."

"Not if I see you in hell first," I force out between clenched teeth.

Not my finest moment, as all it did was elicit a hearty chuckle from her.

"That's the spirit, Marc Sotelo. You'll make a worthy adversary yet," she says before hanging up.

My arm lifts, about to send the phone hurtling through the air, when something else Andrea said registers.

We?

Oh, hell no.

I squeeze my eyes shut, teeth grinding. She had better not be referring to that vile husband of hers. Or her deadbeat son.

Deep, fucking breaths, Marc. I remind myself.

She's not worth it. And if her husband wants to waste his money chasing after ghosts, who am I to stop him? With the dirt I have on the McWhorters, I'll gladly drag their precious name through the mud. By the time I'm done with them, they'll be the laughingstock of this godforsaken town, and I'll be laughing all the way to the fucking bank.

I need Delilah to say the word so that I can reach into the very depths of hell and drag the prodigal daughter back. But not to hand her over to those psychopaths. No, that would be too fucking easy, and I don't *do* easy. If Andrea thinks she will use the twins to reinvent her image as the perfect mother, she's got another think coming.

I draw a slow, laborious breath, force it out through my nostrils, and then set my phone down. Money aside, I don't get what Jordana and Derrick saw in that family. I seriously don't. There aren't any redeeming qualities in that lot, and I've looked. Hard. The Brewer parents weren't materialistic in any way, so there had to be something else that motivated them to accept that stupid deal. And whatever that was, whatever they saw in them eons ago, in Andrea especially, must have since been snuffed out. What's left of them — or rather, in them, despite outward appearances — is a bottomless pit filled with barely disguised anger and resentment for their fuck-ups.

Andrea believes she can force my hand by dangling a path of least resistance before my face, but she conveniently ignores one crucial detail.

I *am* Lorenzo Sotelo's son.

While I'm not actively involved in my father's criminal enterprise, I am apprised of enough details, particularly where the money is involved. That's how I know that the McWhorters have been bleeding money for almost two decades, all because they made a deal with the devil and didn't want to pay her price.

Before they passed away, Matthias's parents hired Olive Hyun to manage some of their investment portfolios. While she's the best at what she does, she likes playing games with people's money. Mathais's parents didn't do their homework before entrusting their wealth to the devil, and that's their damn fault. Had they done so from the start or even read the fucking fine print, they would've known that Olive's specialty is cleaning up blood money for mafia families. If there's even a hint of impropriety with how that wealth was acquired, even if it goes back several generations, Olive will find it and sink her claws into it. That's what she's known for.

It's not that hard to dig up dirt on mafia families. Most of them have skeletons in their metaphorical closets, so they go to Olive in the first place. But it's always the ones with the pristine images that have the most to hide. I don't have the exact details of what she found on the McWhorters, only that it has to do with their obsession with male heirs, and what became of the families of the women who married into the McWhorter family.

I wouldn't say I like throwing the word conspiracy around without any context or facts to back it up, but Olive sure does. And what she found pissed her off, so much such that she fixed it such that Matthias got disinherited in the event of his parent's death, with their wealth being split eighty-twenty between Simone and Curtis.

They thought they could backtrack it by declaring Simon McWhorter legally dead, but that's not how Olive Hyun operates. A death certificate without an actual physical body doesn't change the iron-clad terms of the trust, which Hyun Industries's many subsidiaries are the custodians to this day.

She did plug in a caveat — a middle finger to all of them.

Dead or alive, the Brewer twins will inherit that money on their fortieth birthday. Should anything happen to them, that money goes to charity.

Again, no one thought to read *that* fine print until it was too late.

Dad asked me to take Olive on as a client if the McWhorters came after her for misappropriation of funds. I know that Andrea doesn't want that because a, Olive did exactly what she was hired to do, so they have no case, and b, the last thing they want is for me to aggressively dig up their family's secrets and bring those to light.

Since his parents passed away, Olive has been making Matthias's life financially inconvenient. As a result, he, in turn, can make my life inconvenient by going after the twins. Not only would it be stupid and irresponsible of him to pursue this so-called slave contract, he would be bleeding money they can't afford to lose. If and when that happens, I'll be forced to tell the twins the real reason why Andrea showed them Simone's postcards and why she wants her son back. It all comes down to fucking money.

That won't sit well with Delilah, that's for sure. Or Dahlia, either. They've already lost plenty because of that family.

My sources revealed the McWhorters have been living off Curtis's trust funds, and logic indicates that money will eventually run out. They've had plenty of chances to invest smartly, but they exploit Curtis financially instead. I'll be damned if I let them do the same to Simone and the twins.

A rap on the door cuts through the weighted silence of my thoughts.

It's Harris. It has to be.

Only he would interrupt me in my study. Also, Delilah is passed out in our bed. I put her there after her punishment and aftercare.

"I'm not in the mood," I call out.

There's another rap, and then the unmistakable jingling of the locking mechanism pierces through the silence. The door handle turns and is met with the resistance of the deadbolts.

"Seriously, Marc?"

"What part of go the fuck away did you not understand?"

"I need to talk to you." His plea is gentle, yet it carries a potent torrent of his raw emotions.

I pinch the bridge of my nose and ignore the throbbing ache slowly building in my skull. "Fine. I'm listening."

Another rap. "Preferably face to face."

Huffing out a sigh, I stand and walk over to the door where I hover, my hand hesitating inches away from the highest deadbolt. "No." I slide into a sitting position on the floor, leaning against the wooden surface. "This will have to do."

"That's fair." There's shuffling on his end, and I guess his position mirrors mine on the other side. "What does Andrea want?" is the first question he asks.

"Another audience with the twins." The answer slips out before I have a chance to rein it in. "I told her where to stuff it, not that it's any of your concern. What did you want to talk about?"

A pause ensues. We're not touching, but I can still feel him. I can sense the conflict that rages within him. His guilt bleeds off of him in spades.

Good. Let him sit in that shit. It's only an iota of what Delilah's going through, and he's got it in his head that he can somehow dictate the timeline of her grief. No one has that kind of power over another person's emotions, not even him.

When the silence stretched on for too long, I rise, irritated. "Good talk."

"I didn't know," he says in a desperate tone that shakes my entire being to the core.

A sigh of exasperation moves through me as I return to my position. "Even if you did know, would it have made a difference?"

"Yes." A beat passes, and he blows a breath before amending, "No."

At least he's being honest.

Then he adds, "It isn't healthy, Marc, what she's doing. You know that, right?"

I know that, *and* I understand Harris — probably better than he knows himself.

The thing about Harris is that he's never known the pain of losing that which you love. He's never known just how paralyzing that loss can be.

He's never known what it takes for someone to shut down parts of their brain so that they retain some semblance of a will to live.

It's all because of me.

All my life, I've made it my mission to shield him from that. I made sure he would never know the pain of losing me. I've gone to bat for him with my own family. Mostly because I'm a selfish, possessive fucker who doesn't let go of his things. But also, dead or alive, Harris is it for me.

But things are changing now for all of us. They've been changing ever since Delilah joined our family. It would be naive of us to think we could keep going the way we were. Because, like it or not, Simone is a part of our family. She might not be physically present, but she is emotionally. She always will be, and that's not something he can ignore because her memory is inconvenient for him.

So what if I'm an enabler? Rushing her would do more harm than good.

I would know.

I've had to pick up and piece together the shattered pieces of my own sister's psyche after the damage done to her by both of my parents. At least Courtney has an outlet for her rage. Delilah doesn't have that.

"You've been tracking her cycle for years, H," I remind him. "How could you not know?"

"I stopped doing that months ago."

"How convenient." I don't bother leaving the sarcasm out of my tone.

"Come on, Marc. Don't be mean."

"And stop being an insufferable dick. She's right, you know. The only way this works is if all of us are on board with it, so if you're having second thoughts about kids, you need to speak the fuck up. Your wishy-washy attitude will only drive a wedge between you two."

"I still stand by my words. What she's doing isn't healthy."

"I heard you the first time, H. Re-stating the obvious isn't helping, and if that's all, I have actual work to do."

"You've been in there for hours. Before that, you were in the playroom with her for hours. I made myself scarce like you asked. So, did you smooth things over? Can I talk to her now?"

"That'll have to wait. She asked for punishment when she returned, and her sub-drop lasted longer than the other times. She's asleep now, and I can't have you messing that up."

"So, tomorrow?"

"Absolutely not."

"When—"

"Don't be so pushy, H. It's not a good look for you."

"Neither is this. If you're going to tell me to go pound rocks, at least look me in the fucking face while you do it."

Sliding a knife repeatedly into my chest would be easier than what I'm about to say to him, but it's best to rip *that* bandaid right off, and that needs to be done face-to-face.

Standing, I slide all the deadbolts out of place. By the time I throw open the door, he's standing too.

I take a step toward him. "She's been on a strict regiment of medication for nearly two decades. Did you ever ask her why?"

"I did, once. A long time ago." He takes an answering step toward me, too. "She asked me not to pry, and I'm respecting her wishes."

"That's bullshit, and you know it. You're a doctor, H. I know you can fucking read. When you drugged her eight years ago, you saw how it reacted with her medication."

Something passes through his eyes. Fury, I think. "So we're just supposed to pretend—"

"Yes!" I interject, cutting him off. "If that's what it takes, we'll act like Simone is here. We're going to do that for as long as it takes for D to say the fucking words, and we'll continue doing it until I bring Simone back. You don't like it? Take a fucking hike. Or better yet, leave D the fuck alone. We talked about this months ago, and I don't like repeating myself."

"You mean you talked, and I listened."

"Not hard enough."

"Will you be taking your own advice then?"

"No, I won't, because I fucking love her. I love all of her, not just the parts that suit my needs."

He closes the distance between us and takes my hands in both of his. "I love her too, Marc. I love all of her."

That was never in question. He looks more earnest than I've ever seen him. Still, something about his demeanor seems off.

I lift a curious brow. "Do you? Love her, I mean. Unconditionally."

"Yes, I do. More than you could ever know." His lips come so close to mine that as he speaks, they touch. "And it kills me to see her like this."

I scoff. "You'll live. You're still fucking breathing. You want to act like she's hurting your feelings with this, but you forget that D never lied to you. She never lied to any of us. We're not the center of her universe. We're the consolation prizes she never asked for. The sooner you get that through your head, the easier it will be for you to accept that D won't give Simone up for anyone, not even for you."

He stills before me, eyes searching, expression unreadable. "Nineteen years is a long time, Marc. What happens when she's confronted with the reality she's chasing ghosts?"

"Simone isn't dead. D says so, and I believe her."

"That simple?"

I nod.

"So it's now a shared delusion." He drops my hands and takes a step back. "Fucking great. Let me know when you both come to your senses. In the meantime, I'll look into professional help for *both* of you."

"Do that, and I'll personally kick your ass before she gets a chance to. Use your fucking head, H. There's so much more to this than one legally dead heir, and I'd appreciate it if you would refrain from passing unhelpful judgment on the state of D's mental health. Andrea wouldn't be fighting this hard to bring back a dead body. Dahlia stomached their bullshit for twenty fucking years, so does it make sense that she'd be losing her shit now over some postcards? Why did their parents install military-grade security systems at their house? Ask yourself these questions before you run your mouth about things you know nothing about."

He wraps his arms around his torso, his gaze downcast. "I ask myself all of that, all the time. Delilah doesn't talk to me. Not like she talks to you."

I rake my fingers through my hair. "She has good days and bad days. You've known that for years. She talks to me because I actually listen to her. I don't judge, criticize, or threaten to have her committed every two seconds."

His face lifts to meet mine. "That was never my intention." His voice is raspy, and his eyes burn into me. "I miss her, okay? I miss my best friend. I miss how things used to be between the three of us. Maybe we all need a reset. How about a vacation? We could all use one."

A fucking vacation?

It's my turn to close the gap between us. My hands slide up his chest and loop around his neck. "For once, get out of your fucking head, and see this for what it truly is. D is hurting. She's been hurting for a very long time, and it's not the kind of hurt a fucking vacation will fix. How could you not see that she's been internalizing that hurt for a very long time? They both have. D and Dahlia. But they don't have to do it alone anymore. They have us. We should all do everything we can to understand them and their connection. Sometimes that means walking a mile in their shoes, and it'll be fucking hard. David has known Dahlia for less than a year, yet he's willing to go to the deepest, darkest places of her mind. You've known D for sixteen years, what's your fucking excuse?"

I know it's unfair of me to compare them like that, but my patience is running thin with him.

His jaw shifts from side to side. "Someone has to be the level-headed one in all this."

A pause ensues, fraught with the weight of our shared history. Memories rush in, a bittersweet symphony playing in my mind. Of what we've been through and the storms we've weathered together as a unified front.

"You're it for me, H. You've always been it for me." I close my eyes, press our foreheads together, and take a deep breath before continuing, "But I cannot, no, I will not, sacrifice D's happiness and her mental health to placate this petty jealousy of yours. While D's medication kept her stable all this time, I doubt she properly processed any of the heavy shit that's happened to them — Simone's disappearance, their parent's death, the McWhorter's bullshit, all of it.

"You and I both know she will have to go off of her medications at some point, and it's not the kind you gently wean your body off of. I spoke with Dahlia, and there are no alternatives to what she's on. You saw what pregnancy did to Dahlia. Assume it'll be the same for D, or possibly worse. She knows this too, and still, she wants to do it. Since she'll be putting her body through the fucking wringer so we can grow our family, I don't want to hear your snide comments about how she's doing shit wrong.

"And while you're at it, stop treating her like she's a warm body for you to stick your dick in, and then whine about it when shit doesn't go your way. I'm done playing referee between you two. You're both wrong, but the onus is on you to fix things with her before it's too late. Not today, not tomorrow. In a few days, maybe, and try not to fucking chase her off this time."

With that, my hands fall off his neck and to my sides, and I step out of his embrace. If this is the thing that fractures our unbreakable bond, then so be fucking it.

I'm done with this tedious conversation, and I'm done with his wishy-washy attitude.

So. Fucking. Done.

I head for our bedroom to wrap my arms around the woman who's had me in a chokehold since the day I met her.

13

MARC

The light filters out from underneath our bedroom door and stops me from going in. I press my forehead against the sturdy door, feeling its cool surface against my skin. There's movement on the other side, mostly of papers being shuffled. Then, the unmistakable sound of sniffles cuts through the heavy silence.

Slowly, I turn the doorknob, its metallic protest a soft, reluctant cry. The door opens, revealing Delilah's silhouette bathed in the room's gentle glow. She's seated on the floor with her back to me, but I can still make out the postcards spread out before her.

"You're awake."

She tucks her hands underneath her thighs, hiding them from my view. It's a pointless gesture. I can tell which ones she's studying from their positioning on the floor. She half-turns to face me, and for the second time today, her tear-stained face knocks the air out of my lungs.

I cross the threshold, close the door behind me, and make my way to where she's seated. Crouching before her, I take her shoulders in my hands. "What do you need?"

Her bottom lip trembles slightly, and a knife twists in my chest.

I should have killed Andrea *fucking* McWhorter when I had the chance. As always, that woman is back to her old tricks. She's still messing with my girl, and I don't like it.

And I'm the one who encouraged them to talk with her.

"Just say the word, and it's yours." My plea is gentle, laced with a touch of urgency.

She worries her bottom lip, her gaze dropping to the postcards before us. "It's impossible."

"Nothing is impossible," I remind her, the ache in my chest growing with each passing moment. "Not where I'm concerned."

Without a doubt, I would do anything for her. She makes me want to move heaven and earth to see her smile.

Including this, even if she doesn't ask.

It's my rule. I can bend it anytime I want.

Right now, more than anything, I want to see her smile.

A heavy sigh escapes her lips, followed by a heavy pause, fraught with the weight of the choice she inevitably needs to make.

My heart breaks just a little the longer the silence stretches. Memories rush in, a bittersweet symphony that plays on repeat playing in my mind: laughter, tears, promises — all forged in this very room.

All of which will be upended with four simple words.

"They aren't just postcards," she eventually says, her words carrying a weighty undertone. She brings her hands forward and sets them on the floor before us. "They aren't clues about where she is, just where she's been. These were all places she promised we would go together. She always meant for me to see these, Marc. One way or the other, she knew I would know what these mean. Andrea knew that I would know what these meant. It's no coincidence she's been sitting on them all this time."

"Then why did Dahlia say she'd only return over her parent's dead bodies?"

"That was a smokescreen meant to piss off Matthias. It's safe to say it worked." Her face lifts, and her lips stretch into a sad smile.

I return the favor, my eyes searching hers. "Say the words, D."

"I'll do you one better." She pulls out her book from where it's tucked underneath her thigh and hands it to me. On page one, the four words are written in bold letters.

I want her back.

Fucking finally.

EPILOGUE

SIMONE

Present Day

The afternoon air carries a faint promise of new beginnings as I stand at the threshold of my new house. Goosebumps litter my clothed arms, a sordid confirmation that the frigid Midwest winter is finally over. It's time to embrace the spring, and

At least I don't have to winter-proof my new home. It's one less thing to worry about on the list of a gazillion other things that need to be done.

On the outside, it's a beautiful structure — a ranch-style home with a wrap-around faux brick façade and towering windows that seem to welcome the sunlight. It's also a cookie-cutter house that looks like every other house on the block.

In other words, it's unassuming, like its previous owner. And inconspicuous, like me.

"Holy shit, this thing is still here," CC exclaims as she pulls out a penny-sized pebble and triumphantly holds it up. "Oscar shoved it in there the day I moved in."

That would be her husband, Oscar, who walks into the room with his arms full of crumpled-up bedsheets. "I was going to toss these in the wash, but I'll take them with me to save you the trouble."

"You know you don't have to do that, right? I can make my bed and do my laundry."

He waves me off. "Nonsense. Your new bed will be here within the hour. It's the least I could do."

"I don't need a new bed. That one works just fine."

"Trust me, you do." He angles his chin at the front door. "My Mistress gave me a job to do, and I'm very thorough."

I shake my head as he waltzes past me and to their car outside, barefoot with the sheets in his arms.

For Midwest weather in April, he must have a death wish. Still, it's better than what happened on Christmas day. He even has most of his clothing on this time, not just his boxers.

Courtney tasked him with taking apart the master bedroom; something about him combing through the room for any lingering traces of them. It's a pointless task, and she only assigned that to him to provoke his bratty side; that way, she'd have a reason to punish him. She's a Domme with a sadistic streak that rivals my own, and what do you know? Oscar is a fucking masochist, and CC dishes it as good as she gets.

Succinctly put, it's a match made in kink heaven.

However, Courtney didn't count on him being the perfect sub for the day, complying with her every request, no matter how asinine. I suspect it's because CC bribed him ahead of time... and most likely stuck a vibrating anal plug into his ass.

The dynamics between those three certainly keep things interesting.

"Thanks again for helping me move in," I call out after him.

"Are you kidding? I wouldn't miss this for the world." Oscar's energy is infectious, and his presence brings out an instant surge of reassurance in me.

I should explain why that is. Courtney, CC, and Oscar are a throuple. He and CC got married last December, and then they both took Courtney's last name, Bardales Sotelo and are enjoying happily wedded bliss. It's been a long and bumpy road to their happy ever after, and if anyone deserves a win, it's these three.

That, and I bought CC's old place from her. After she and Oscar moved in with Courtney last winter, this place collected dust. She won't admit it, but I'm pretty sure Courtney talked CC into convincing me to take this house off her hands. CC doesn't care about money; it's more like Abby — my other friend — was running out of inconspicuous places to stash me.

This place, however, is meant to be a new beginning for me — a clean slate of sorts.

It doesn't mean the sheets have to be tossed or the bed needs to be replaced, though. But Courtney gave the order, so who am I to argue?

"I still can't believe you want to live here," Roxane says as she lines dishes up on the kitchen island. "It defeats the purpose of staying in the shadows."

"Or it's genius," CC still takes credit for this, and I'm inclined to let her. "It's the last place anyone would think to look."

"Including the twins?" Roxane chimes.

The mention of their names sends a nostalgic pang piercing through my heart.

"Especially the twins," CC asserts. "They have no reason to. I don't live here anymore. Besides, you insisted that the deed to the house be registered in Oscar's name for now, so as far as anyone's concerned, I gave my husband a gift."

The hardest part about living as a ghost is having to watch the ones you left behind grieve your loss and then watch them move on with their lives. It's what I wanted for them in the first place, so my wish came through, albeit decades later and with several strings attached.

If anyone had told me then that I'd someday buy a house and establish roots in one place, I'd have laughed in their face, stabbed them in the jugular, and then set their corpse on fire because I'm nice like that. I'm also thorough, too. It's in my best interest not to leave trace evidence behind; nothing does the job better than fire does.

They don't call me Phoenix for nothing.

Fire can be a formidable weapon if you know what you're doing. Nitric acid does the job, but the nickname Lady Poison doesn't quite have the same ring. It's why I ditched that moniker years ago.

So why did I get the need to settle down now, after so much time has passed?

Four reasons.

I have a score to settle, an empire to topple, a celebratory bonfire to host, and a promise to make good on.

Now, I have to deal with the added complication of Courtney's brother siccing Diabolus on my tail. It pissed Abby off, and it's been amusing to watch the lengths to which those two hackers will go to get under each other's skin. All in good fun, of course. So far, Abby's winning, but Diabulous could tip those scales at any time.

My take is that if Diabolus is going to find me, it needs to be on my turf and on my terms.

For nearly two decades, my motto has been simple.

Stay off everyone's radar.

This is anything but.

Anxiety flits through me, intertwining with excitement as I step back to let in my friends, Courtney and Abby, each carrying a box of books.

"Where do you want these?" Abby asks, huffing out a breath.

I point to the cardboard boxes lining the walls, awaiting their purpose. "Over there. There's less of a chance Charlie will get into those."

"Hah, you wish," Courtney chuckles as she sets down her box, then looks around. "It's too quiet in here. Where are the little buggers, anyway?"

"In the main bedroom," I tell her. "Oscar took Charlie and Tiffany in there, promising them the biggest pillow fort they've ever seen."

"Ah. I call it the Oscar-special." She smiles and wipes her hands on her jeans. "He tricked them into napping by making it a game. It's fucking genius. I should've married him a long time ago."

"You did not just say that," CC exclaims, then tosses a throw pillow in her direction.

Courtney effortlessly swats it away, and the next thing I know, she and CC are rolling around in the middle of the room, in a tangle of legs and arms, with punctuated pauses for making out. Oscar returns at some point, looks at them, and opts to join Roxane at the kitchen island instead.

It's good seeing them like this. It's rare for Courtney to lower her guard like this completely, but CC has a knack for coaxing out her playful side. Seeing them like this takes me back to a simpler time, a cherished memory of the three amigos flits to the forefront of my mind.

When I walked away from everyone I knew and loved nineteen years ago, I never expected to gain new ones along the way. This life has been full of surprises, and it's only a matter of time before my past and present come full circle.

Unbeknownst to me, fate had already set the wheels into motion eighteen months ago — a chance meeting that resulted in my niece; all

I can do now is ride it out while simultaneously checking off my decades in the making bucket list.

That can be tomorrow's problem. Today, amid the chaos and laughter, I'm grateful for these friends who've turned a daunting task into another cherished memory.

Warm breath fans over my shoulder seconds before a hand touches my back, running soothingly up and down my spine. "Don't pay them any mind," Abby whispers, pressing her lips against my shoulder.

"Hmm," I hum a response. "I'm enjoying the show."

And it's better the alternative.

"Right," "Abby drawls as she hooks a finger underneath my chin and forces my face to hers. "Is that why you're shaking?"

Hmm.

My gaze lowered to my arms, confirming what I'd already suspected. I remind myself that this isn't real. It's just my body's involuntary reaction to memories of my soulmate and of what once was, flitters to the forefront of my mind.

"It's not a big deal," I mumble, meeting Abby's dark brown eyes. "It'll pass like, it always does."

Her eyes twinkle in the afternoon light, and the corners of her lips turn up. Without context, anyone watching would mistake this for romantic interest, but Abby and I have zero chemistry.

We do have other things in common, though. Like a shared love of science, and an insatiable drive for revenge and justice — our version of it, anyway. Ours is a strictly intellectual attraction, not a physical one.

"It's not nice of you to use me to make Roxane jealous," I remind her as my gaze darts over to Roxane's and Oscar's eyes glued to us instead of the more entertaining scene before them. A curious smile plays on Oscar's lips, while a glossy sheen appears in Roxane's. Under different circumstances, I couldn't care less, but this is one complicated love triangle I do not want to be caught in the middle of. A resigned sigh moves through me as my eyes meet Abby's dead-on. "She already knows nothing is going on between us. Then there's the matter of—"

"Hey, hands off!" Courtney scolds, cutting me off. Usually, she'd add the words *my pet* at the end of that sentence, but she's been intentional about leaving that off with the present company.

Something tells me her romantic partners haven't been brought up to speed on *that* aspect of our relationship either.

Abby chuckles, and her hands fall to her sides as she steps back. "Yes, boss," she says, knowing it would piss Courtney off.

I, on the other hand, mumble, "Yes, Mistress," under my breath.

It's too low for anyone to hear, but Courtney can fucking read lips too. Her eyes briefly narrow in annoyance, then she's back to kissing her wife to distract her from that exchange.

See, in addition to living as a ghost for nearly two decades, I've also been under the protection of the Sotelo crime family. And even though Courtney and I are friends *now*, we didn't start that way.

We started as Owner and slave, and that aspect of our relationship hasn't changed.

Succinctly put, I'm her pet.

Her human pet, but still a pet nonetheless, and it would do me well to always remember that.

It keeps my eye on the prize, a harsh reminder that through no fault of theirs, Dahlia and Delilah Brewer legally belong to the McWhorter family. It's a promise that, come hell or high water, that's a legal bond I intend to sever.

To truly walk a mile in the twin's shoes, I was locked into a similar contract.

And for me to break free of it, the McWhorter empire must crumble.

Sounds simple, right?

It's anything but.

As far as I know, her brother — whom she's categorically and repeatedly declared is off-limits to me — is unaware of my affiliation with the Sotelo crime family.

Specifically, Marc has been kept in the dark about Simone McWhorter's affiliation with his family. Lorenzo made the call to keep that from him, and nineteen years is a long fucking time to keep that under wraps.

But Marc is smart, and it's only a matter of time before he pieces together that Phoenix and Simone McWhorter are the same person.

Then again, he knew his sister had pets in the past, courtesy of Daddy Dearest, and he also knew what became of those pets.

I would know. I've dissolved enough of those in lye and flushed them down the drain.

On Courtney's orders, of course.

As I said, her sadistic streak rivals my own, and I'm pretty ruthless.

I have to be, seeing as I plan on tearing apart the bloody foundations of the family I was born into. It's the only way my soulmates would be free of our tenuous bond.

Eye on the fucking prize.

Always.

———

To be continued in
In Plain Sight
(*Sin and Sinuosity Book 4*)

Some feelings never fade with time.
They only grow stronger. Brighter. Deadlier.

When faced with an impossible choice, I made the gut-wrenching decision to sever ties with everything and everyone I held dear — my friends, my family, and even the person I loved more than life itself.
To the world, it was a tragic tale of love and loss.
Little did they know, it was all a twisted fabrication — a web of deceit, a tapestry of lies, and betrayal that was intricately woven into the very core of my existence.
Into our existence.
Soulmates or not, walking away was the only logical path, a tragic necessity and a painful step towards an inevitable, bitter conclusion.
Embracing life in the shadows became a bearable solace, a means to exact vengeance on the malevolent forces who tainted our very essence from the start.
But fate had its own sinister plans, as did the ones I left behind.
The ones who still hold a piece of my heart.
Now, as the past resurfaces and secrets unravel, the burning question remains: is love truly eternal, or are some loves doomed to a far more sinister fate?

Coming February 2024
Available for Pre-order:
https://elicenange.com/inplainsight/

THANK YOU!

Thank you for reading PROMISE ME FOREVER, and I hope you enjoyed this little snippet of Delilah's, Harris's, and Marc's story.

This book is a labor of love, and I'd appreciate it if you left a review on as many platforms as possible.

Want more on this trio?
Visit my website for Bonus Content and Deleted Scenes:
https://elicenange.com/bonuscontent/

If you want to stay up to date on news about new releases and sneak peaks of new books, sign up for my newsletter:
https://elicenange.com/newsletter/

TASTE OF HELL

Hell isn't fire and brimstone; it's the secrets you keep.

DAHLIA

Prestige, pedigree, old money. What should have been a privilege felt more like slavery.

A cage made up of old family secrets. Ones so terrible I was willing to sacrifice it all to keep my identical twin sister from being owned like me.

My sister and I were born miracles and forced to be celebrities because of it. The media dubbed my sister as *defective* and myself as some kind of living *perfection*.

If they only knew I was the truly damaged one here. If they only knew bad things can happen to miracles too.

Forced to pick up the broken pieces of my life when I refused to play by their rules, I stopped living up to their delusions.

When I hired *David Holcomb* for a night it was purely business; *I wasn't supposed to fall for the hired help.*

DAVID

Heartache, lies, all the blood on my hands. Life has always been a little taste of hell.

Most women could smell the troubled past on me and it made my job pretty easy.

The women who hired me always seemed to think if they moaned loud enough it would silence all the bad things in my head. Except *Dahlia Brewer*.

Maybe it was because we were using each other as some kind of freedom.

She had something I needed; *I didn't know that would be her.*

Start Reading **TASTE OF HELL**, Book 1 of the ***Sin and Sinuosity*** series today:

https://elicenange.com/tasteofhell/

ACKNOWLEDGMENTS

It takes a village. Truly.

1. My family, Mr. Nange and ~~Baby~~ Toddler Nange. Thank you for all your love and support as I navigate through this exciting yet risky publishing journey.
2. My critique partner, Stephanie Quinn. Even though you only say 1% of this book, your feedback was invaluable.
3. My *other* critique partner, Anonymous – thank you for indulging me and all of my crazy, haphazard ideas. I do have a lot of those, don't I? Then again, you have a knack for keeping me on track with all of these, so thank you — from the bottom of my heart.
4. My beta reader, Deb Peach. Thank you for taking on this trio's story at such short notice. All of your suggestions on how to make the story stronger have been invaluable, so thank you!
5. Leanne Rabesa, my editor. For that encyclopedia brain of yours, amongst other things. Your insightful comments often crack me up, as well as your ability to understand these darn characters even better than I do!
6. Renita McKinney, my sensitivity editor. Where have you been all my life?! I'm glad we connected last year; and thrilled you took apart this book and **Touch Of Heaven** on such short notice… even though it took me forever (pun intended) to polish up this part for release.
7. My inspirations. Since all three of you are still choosing to remain anonymous, I'm acknowledging you anyway. Anonymously. We still have a few more books left in this series, so this isn't going anywhere :)

8. Last but not least – to you, lovely reader, who's reading this. Thank you for coming on this wild journey with me. Hope you stick around. There's more where this came from!

BOOKS BY ELICE NANGE

Sin and Sinuosity series

Taste Of Hell

Touch Of Heaven

Six Feet Under

Promise Me Forever

In Plain Sight (Book 4) - *2/2024*

Novellas

Twist Our Hearts (Book 0.5) - Pre-order, Summer 2024

Six Feet Dark (Book 2.5) - Pre-order, Summer *2024*

ABOUT THE AUTHOR

Elice Nange is a Contemporary and Dark Romance author. She writes from the heart, and her stories often address sensitive subjects like racism, sexual orientation, discrimination, etc.

Outside of writing, she enjoys spending time with her family and copious amounts of reading. She is also obsessed with Maya Angelou, ice cream, and the color purple ~ not necessarily in that order.
www.elicenange.com

facebook.com/elicenange
x.com/elicenange
instagram.com/elicenange
tiktok.com/@elicenange

AFTERWORD

Musings of a delicatesoul88

It still feels so surreal that this is the fourth (or is it the fifth?) installment of this series. I also say this every time because it's the god-honest truth. If I say it enough times, I'll come to believe it someday. So, in keeping with the previous three books, let's call this one The Making of **Promise Me Forever** as well. It's more like the making of **Touch Of Heaven: Extended Edition** since that's technically what this was.

Also, this is my jumbled-up ramblings and my unedited, un-prettified things thoughts, so it's obviously not proofread, nor does it follow the quote-on-quote, 'standard' rules of punctuation. But you're still reading past this sentence anyway, so I assume you are still just as interested in reading this as I am writing this. I don't know why you all read it or why you are interested in it, but it's fun to write, so here goes nothing!

This one was a tough one to write. Then again, Delilah has always been a challenge to write. Dahlia, too, to be honest. Funny story — half of this was meant to be the ending to **Touch Of Heaven** (hence the Extended Edition tag above). The phrase "I want her back" was meant to close out that book. As you can see, this ending is as vague and open-ended as it gets, and my intention with each full-length book in this series is for it to be a standalone. It is an interconnected standalone, but a standalone nonetheless.

If you read this and thought — hmm… of this trio, Harris is actually making sense, and the rest of them need professional help; then your intuition is on the right track. I write dark romance (and I read a lot of it too). To me, dark doesn't necessarily mean blood and guts and gore. It could also mean the deepest, darkest places our minds go to. What Delilah is doing isn't healthy, and she romanticizes Simone quite a bit. That romanticism has since morphed over the years, and she's on the brink of madness with her obsession. Don't get me wrong, she's in love with Marc and Harris, but she's also using them (and they're using her right back).

To Marc, *I want her back* could only mean one thing, and Delilah knows that. I'd like to think there's a part of her that understands just because she wants her legally dead (ex-) girlfriend back doesn't necessarily mean that's who she'll be getting back. Nineteen-year-old Simone and Thirty-eight-year-old Simone are obviously different, and if you read **Six Feet Under**, you'd know — she's all over that book and I wasn't being subtle about it. I can't wait to see how that unfolds! It's my first time truly delving into the Forced Proximity trope, and it's a blast!

I've teased Simone's story for long enough, and it's her turn next. I'm in the thick of writing In Plain Sight now, and let's just say it is as dark and depraved as I envisioned. It's on track for its February 2024 release, and I can't wait to start sharing teasers and excerpts in 2024.

Before I sign off (and before our imaginations run wild), I should clarify two major plot points with this series. **Yes**, Derrick, Jordana, and Andrea used to be a thing when they were younger (it ended before the twins were born). **No**, Derrick is **not** Simone's or Curtis's biological father. Derrick was infertile as a direct result of some messed-up shit that happened to him as a child. It's why he went into research in the first place. The twins were conceived via IVF, using the sperm of an anonymous donor. **No**, I'm not throwing in any more conspiracies as to who this anonymous donor was (it's tempting, though), but trust me, we already have enough conspiracies going on with the series. We don't need to tack on anymore… or do we?

Just kidding, we don't. We really don't. And since I've rambled long enough, so bye now! In the meantime, stay overly ambitious.

Elice Nange